Growing Pains

Growing Pains

Ian Whates

2013

GROWING PAINS
Copyright © Ian Whates 2013

COVER ART
Copyright © Tomislav Tikulin 2013

Published in April 2013 by PS Publishing Ltd. by arrangement with the author. All rights reserved by the author. The right of Ian Whates to be identified as Author of this Work has been asserted by him in accordance with the Copyright, Designs and Patents Act 1988.

FIRST PS EDITION

ISBN
978-1-848636-00-2
978-1-848636-01-9 (signed edition)

This book is a work of fiction. Names, characters, places and incidents either are products of the author's imagination or are used fictitiously. Any resemblance to actual events or locales or persons, living or dead, is entirely coincidental.

"Growing Pains", first appeared in *Hub*, October 2009; "The Assistant", *Solaris Book of New SF 3*, ed George Mann, Solaris, 2009; "Walking the Dog", *Bards and Sages*, April 2009; "Morphs", *In Bad Dreams II*, ed Sharyn Lilley, Eneit Press, 2009; "Peeling an Onion", *Forgotten Worlds*, July 2006; "A Question of Timing", previously unpublished; "Coffee Break", *Hub*, January 2008; "The Outsider", *Under the Rose*, ed Dave Hutchinson, Norilana Books, 2009; "Hobbies", previously unpublished; "Shop Talk", *Warrior Women II*, ed Roby James, Norilana Books, 2009; "The Piano Song", *Scenes from the Second Storey*, ed Mark Deniz, Morrigan Books, 2011.

Design & Layout by Michael Smith
Printed and bound in England by the MPG Books Group

PS Publishing Ltd
Grosvenor House
1 New Road
Hornsea, HU18 1PG
England

editor@pspublishing.co.uk | www.pspublishing.co.uk

Contents

1 . . . . Growing Pains

15 . . . . The Assistant

31 . . . . Walking the Dog

35 . . . . Morphs

49 . . . . Peeling an Onion

59 . . . . A Question of Timing

67 . . . . Coffee Break

75 . . . . The Outsider

87 . . . . Hobbies

95 . . . . Shop Talk

113 . . . . The Piano Song

GROWING PAINS

I WAS UP EARLY THAT PARTICULAR SATURDAY; I mean *really* early. It was having Rachel and her family staying that did it. I'd been on tenterhooks from the moment, late on Friday afternoon, when their silver Merc picked its way gingerly along the narrow lane and drew up outside the house. Don't get me wrong, I love my sister and Geoff's okay, she could have done a lot worse. Come to think of it, she *had* done a lot worse—I remember her first husband.

The problem was not even that she was a city girl through and through. Okay, so she thought I was crazy to have turned my back on the rat race and taken up fruit farming in the back-of-beyond, but hell, I could hardly blame her for that. Half the time I agreed with her.

No, it was the timing of their visit that was the problem. Looking back, perhaps I should have been firmer, but I'd already put them off so often they were beginning to take offence. I suppose secrets do that—create tension where none belongs and cast the shadow of anxiety over normal interactions, even with family. David was my main worry. It was hard to remember sometimes with all that had happened of late, but he was still just a kid. Could he really be expected to go the whole weekend without letting something slip, without giving us away?

To date Rachel just *thought* I was crazy. I preferred to keep it that way.

Then, of course, there was my niece, Jude—she refused to answer to 'Judith'. Jude was eight months older than David and in theory having another child around of similar age seemed like a good idea. In practice the veneer of their apparent common interests hid a chasm of differences. They both loved music: she was into chart stuff while he was addicted to sub-genres I'd never even heard of, but which sounded to

GROWING PAINS

me like grunge and new metal. They both loved virtual reality games: she enjoyed creating virtual families and designing their virtual homes, while he enjoyed blowing things up. They were both into clothes: she loved to dress up and he took delight in dressing down. They both loved the outdoors, but he was inquisitive and never happier than when getting down and dirty, while she preferred her countryside sanitised—preferably viewed from the back of a horse . . . and we never have owned a horse.

There was also David's love of all things mechanical, particularly anything that vaguely resembled a weapon. He was rarely to be seen without a toy gun of some sort in his hand, often taking aim at someone or other. During that particular weekend, the designated 'someone' was invariably Jude. Rachel had already made a couple of comments about the need for a 'feminine influence' and my son's 'worrying violent tendencies.' My dismissal of such concerns with 'he's only playing' seemed to cut very little ice and I was hardly in a position to explain that I actually *encouraged* such play, or to explain the reasons why.

Add to the mix the fact that one was a boy and the other a girl and you were left with two surly kids who would rarely acknowledge each other's existence without being bullied into doing so. None of which helped make the weekend any easier.

It was still dark when I tip-toed downstairs and went into the kitchen to make a cup of tea. The unforgiving stone floor radiated a slight chill that seeped up through the soles of my bare feet, and I was glad to retreat to the comparative warmth of the lounge carpet.

David's alarm was set to wake him in little over an hour. Hopefully we could be out of the house before anyone else even realised we were up.

I settled into my favourite chair, switched on the standard lamp and tried to read; failing dismally for the most part, my thoughts constantly straying onto other matters. When sounds of muffled movement finally came from upstairs I had managed no more than a couple of pages, and they would need to be reread.

I rose and headed back into the kitchen, without bothering to check the time. Then something prompted me to pause and listen more closely.

Over the years I'd grown accustomed to the rhythm of David's footfalls, the sound of his rummaging, and this didn't *sound* like him moving around up there.

Sure enough, the figure that appeared seconds later was far too large to be my son.

Geoff; his tall, broad-shouldered frame seeming to fill the entire stairwell. So much for sneaking out unnoticed.

"Morning. You're up early."

I winced at the unrestrained boom and wondered fleetingly whether 'Geoffs' came with any form of volume control.

Some level of disapproval must have registered on my face, because he waved a hand dismissively, saying, "Don't worry about Rach—she'll be asleep for hours yet. And as for Jude, it would take a bomb going off to wake her up."

No concern for disturbing David, I noticed.

Not that it mattered; I could already hear more movement—the protest of disturbed bedsprings, like the warning of some far-off thunder storm, and the creak of trodden floorboards. Seconds later, a dishevelled bundle of pre-adolescent energy came hurtling down the stairs to vanish into the cloakroom, a stage-whispered, "Hi, Dad," trailing in its wake.

Geoff observed the mini-typhoon's passage with a wry smile and then proved that he *could* moderate his voice when it suited him, saying in subdued tone, "He's a great credit to you, you know. It can't have been easy since Susan left."

My response was some meaningless platitude or other. I hate talking about Susan, almost as much as I hate thinking about her.

The three of us sat down to breakfast in the kitchen, with David unusually quiet. He clearly realised that Uncle Geoff's presence was not part of the plan and kept glancing in my direction as if imploring me to do something. I ran through various possibilities in my mind as the haphazard pile of toast—which started out resembling some roughly-built cavalry fort in an old Hollywood western—was steadily demolished, log by log, and cereal bowls were wiped clean. By the time we'd finished, David's furtive glances had gained an edge of desperation.

"Right then," I said, pushing my chair back from the table and standing up. "Are you all set, David?" Without waiting for a reply, I turned to Geoff; "Don't worry about washing up the breakfast things, I'll see to them when we get back."

"Where are you off to?"

"Just a few bits and pieces that need doing; we won't be long."

"Work? But it's the weekend."

GROWING PAINS

I smiled, hoping it didn't come across as too patronising. "You're in the countryside now, Geoff. Things don't take a break from growing on Friday night and put their feet up till Monday. They keep right on going all through the weekend."

"Sure, but I thought with us here... I mean, you haven't seen Rachel or Jude in... what, six months?"

"At least. But this is a working farm. It's how David and I earn a living and it's a critical time of year right now; the strawberries are just about there and we'll be opening up for pick-your-own next weekend. We can't afford to neglect them."

He seemed to absorb that for a second. "Okay, point taken. Guess I'll tag along with you, then."

No! Somehow I managed to avoid voicing the protest, although the look of horror on David's face shouted it effectively enough. Fortunately Geoff was completely oblivious.

"No need," I said, as casually as I could manage. "It's just boring, routine stuff."

"Fine. Rachel's always saying I should take more interest in what you guys do around here."

His mind was clearly made up and nothing I said would deter him. Short of being rude or physically tying him to a chair, we were going to have to accept his company and just pray for an uneventful morning. David had produced a gun from somewhere and was running around mock-shooting his Uncle Geoff from every conceivable angle.

I knew exactly how he felt.

It was a tight squeeze with three of us in the cab—neither Geoff nor I are small men—and today the truck seemed determined to find every bump in the dirt-track that masqueraded as an unmade road. The three of us jolted and shook in unison, like a trio of plastic monkeys fused at the sides and sculpted by a single mould. Fortunately the ride was a short one.

"Whatever happened to walking?" Geoff wanted to know. "I thought this was supposed to be the healthy life; didn't realise you just jump in a car to go off to work like the rest of us."

"It's a truck, not a car," David snapped peevishly as we drew to a stop.

It was a lovely morning—the sort that should explain far better than any argument of mine precisely why we had abandoned the City. I have no idea whether or not Geoff even noticed.

The first thing I heard on climbing down from the cab was the song of a skylark. The fact that it was already aloft so early in the day spoke volumes for just how warm it was. I glanced up and tried to spot the bird. Normally the sound drifts down from on-high like the song of an unseen angel, but today I saw it immediately—a tiny speck on-the-wing, voicing its glory.

Rather than being an isolated voice, the lark was more a soloist, its song set against the background chorus of other birds declaring their presence and their territory. Even Geoff paused to listen and it occurred to me that being born and bred in the blandness of suburbia he might never have heard a *real* dawn chorus before.

The sun's nimbus was just clearing the hedgerow. If anything was going to happen, it would be in the next few minutes. I found myself increasingly on edge and hoped my anxiety didn't convey itself to Geoff.

David and I helped each other wriggle into our harnesses with practiced ease.

Geoff looked on, bemused. "And those are for . . . ?" he asked, indicating the cumbersome plastic containers we now had strapped to our backs, both heavy with water.

"Watering the fruit," I explained. I tested the pressurised gun that fed off the tank. Satisfied, I looked up to find David already a few rows away, eager to begin. At my nod, we set off. Geoff accompanied me as we walked up the central avenue. Rows of strawberry plants radiated off to right and left, the plants sitting proud on their straw-topped mounds; flashes of red amongst the green, yellow and brown.

"Rachel tells me you're expanding the 'pick-your-own' side of things," he said.

"Yes. In addition to the soft fruit—raspberries, blackcurrants and the two varieties of strawberry—we thought we'd give some vegetables a go this year." I was talking on automatic pilot, most of my attention focussed on scanning the edge of the field. I knew without looking that David was doing the same a few rows away. "So we've got peas, beans, mange tout, cauliflower and cabbage."

"Why two types of strawberry?"

I had explained all this before, realising from his glazed expression at the time that it was going in one ear and out the other. "One's a June bearing variety. They produce the best crop but only fruit once each year—in late spring/early summer."

GROWING PAINS

"Now, in other words."

"Right. The other is an ever-bearing strain, which fruits again in the autumn, giving us a second crack at the strawberry-loving public. There's less demand at that time of the year but also less competition, so the smaller crop works well."

The conversation was helping to divert him from pondering any awkward questions, such as why David and I had yet to spray a single drop of water from the heavy tanks we insisted on lugging around.

I caught a blinding flash over Geoff's shoulder, as if sunlight had glanced off a reflective surface straight into my eyes. My heart sank. *Why today of all days?* David spotted it too and was already scampering towards it. I steered Geoff in the same direction at a more leisurely pace, trying not to be too obvious. Absurd really—he was hardly going to remain unaware for much longer, but it seems that secrecy is a habit we cling to until the bitter end.

Another flash; right beside me this time. Geoff's startled hop backwards and exclamation of "What the . . . ?" would have been comical in other circumstances.

I ignored him and concentrated on the bolter. It had touched down at the start of a row, as they invariably tend to, then instantly arced to hit another plant two or three removed from the first before jumping to the next row and a further plant. This all occurred in a split second, the impression of a bridge of light more visual after-image than anything actually seen. I reacted instantly, raising my 'gun' and sending a stream of water in pursuit. Too slow. The bolter had already moved on, continuing its dance down the row. Wherever it touched, the strawberry plants were left unharmed but stripped of fruit.

A second stream of water intersected the bolter's path. There was a loud crack, reminiscent of a fire-cracker going off, and a blinding flare of light, accompanied by a young boy's triumphant roar of "Yes!" The bolter was gone. Thank God for David. My reactions are pretty good but my son's are a fraction faster, presumably because he's that much younger. When things happen at this speed, a fraction makes all the difference.

"What the hell was that?" Fear or shock made Geoff's question overloud and angry.

I held up a restraining hand as he went to step forward from the central avenue. "Don't come between the rows. You don't want to be touched by one of these things and you've seen how quickly they can arc across." The fact that David and I were standing between rows was something I did not need reminding of. We were both in a position to defend ourselves.

Even as I finished speaking it began again. Multiples this time; I didn't stop to count how many. I fired instinctively... and missed. Crack, flash and cheer to my left told me that David had been more successful. One came hopping down the row towards me, like some mischievous imp of light. I tried to gauge where it would be rather than where it was, squeezed off a jet of water and got lucky, but there was another immediately behind it.

There ensued a brief period of chaos: bolts of light dazzling the periphery of vision, jets of water missing, hitting, flares and small explosions, whoops of childish delight, spots dancing before my eyes and trousers that were somehow soaked through by the end. As ever, I gained an impression of vitality and purpose from these small, self-contained bolts of energy, but no real indication of whether or not they were even aware of us.

Suddenly it was over, leaving me with the vague sense of a task unfinished. I stood there, breathing hard, adrenaline still pumping, waiting for the next wave, but none came.

David gave an exultant cheer as the realisation sunk in that this really was the end and not simply a pause. "I got twelve," he declared proudly. "How many did you get, Dad?"

"Five." Well, four that I was certain of and a fifth that both of us had gone for at the same time.

I looked around and knew the relief of success. In our immediate vicinity the strawberry crop had vanished, the plants stripped bare, but the affected area was mercifully small. We'd succeeded in containing the bolters to the corner where they had come through on this occasion. Unchecked, an incursion like this would have stripped the field of fruit in a matter of minutes. If even one bolter had slipped past it would have been a disaster. But none had.

"So what on Earth was that all about?"

I couldn't help it, I laughed. The release of tension and the return to the mundane encompassed in Geoff's question set me off. "I'm sorry, Geoff."

"Bolters," David supplied as I brought myself under control. "As in lightning bolts."

GROWING PAINS

"Those were *not* lightning bolts," Geoff stated emphatically.

"No, you're right," I agreed, composure restored, "but that's what we call them: bolters." I knew nothing about them when I bought the place—I don't think anybody who comes into fruit farming from the outside ever does. A trade secret, so to speak.

Geoff crouched down to examine one of the plants whose fruit had been harvested during the raid. "I thought it was going to be burnt," he murmured, "but there's not a mark on it."

"I know. Clever little devils, aren't they?"

"But *what* are they?"

"Self-contained, animate parcels of energy," I explained. "They're electrical in nature and they love soft fruit." Two sentences which encapsulated virtually everything about bolters that anyone was certain of.

"Self contained...? They just looked like short lightning bolts, anchored between plants, bending and... I mean, it's not possible."

"Yes, I went to the same sort of physics lessons you did," I assured him. "You're right, bolters ought to be impossible, but..."

"They just appeared out of nowhere." He really was struggling with this, unable or unwilling to accept what his eyes had reported. "They must have come from *somewhere*."

"But not from here."

"What do you mean?"

"Aliens," David chipped in gleefully.

"Oh come on!"

"Think about it," I said. "They contravene every law of science we were ever taught, yet clearly they exist—so wherever they come from their existence *isn't* an impossibility, it's a fact. And wherever *that* is, it's not here."

"Yes, but... aliens? Where's their space ship?"

"They don't need one. I don't think they come from 'up there' at all," I waved vaguely at the heavens. This was where things got a little tricky. I took a deep breath. "Membrane theory." Just because I was a fruit farmer didn't mean I'd entirely lost touch with such things.

Geoff looked blank and shook his head.

"It's a theory which supposes that we're just one of an infinite number of multiple realities existing in parallel with one another. I think the bolters come from one of the others, or maybe exist between realities, crossing several in the search of food." In my mind I had the image of vast swarms of bolters floating in the gaps between, creatures of the void that were drawn to any place where they sensed sustenance, able to cross into different realities when conditions allowed.

"You don't honestly believe all this nonsense, do you?"

"You've seen the bolters; got any better ideas?"

There was silence while he mulled it over. You could almost see the cogs turning beneath his furrowed brow. "So when you spray them with water..."

"We don't know for certain." I shrugged. "There's a release of energy and they vanish. Perhaps that means we've killed them..."

"Course we've killed them," David interrupted

"... or perhaps the water shorts something out and simply snaps them back to wherever it is they come from," I continued. "To be honest, it's anyone's guess. And do you know something else?"

"What?"

"I really couldn't care less."

"But..."

I held up a hand to forestall whatever he was about to say and spoke over him—I was starting to lose patience. "Look, Geoff, we're not even sure these things are alive. They could be constructs for all we know—machines of some sort sent here to harvest the fruit for unseen masters, or they might be mindless creatures with a sweet tooth who've evolved an instinctive means of crossing dimensions to feed. If they *are* alive, there's never been any indication they're sentient. All anyone has ever seen is a mindless drive to devour fruit and sometimes a reaction to avoid water. Hunger and self preservation, two of the most basic instincts you could wish for. But I still know exactly what they are."

"Which is?" he asked on cue.

"Vermin; inter-dimensional fruit-eating vermin. And we know what to do with vermin, don't we David?"

"Shoot them!" He yelled with such enthusiasm that Geoff looked deeply shocked, which caused a broad grin to break through despite my best efforts. Geoff could be a real tight-ass on occasion and I was rather enjoying seeing his world view shaken a little.

He and I returned to the truck, while David headed off to do one more circuit of the field, just in case. There was unlikely to be any more

GROWING PAINS

trouble that morning—assuming the bolters stuck to their familiar pattern—but it would help him to burn off some excess energy and calm down a little following the raid.

"You're going to have to report this, you know," Geoff said, once we were both in the cab.

I shook my head. "No point. It's been tried before. A grower reported it back in the 80s, apparently."

"It's been going on that long?"

I nodded. "So I'm told."

"What happened?"

"He was ridiculed and dismissed as a crackpot. Presumably people still had all that fuss about crop circles fresh in their minds."

"Hardly surprising if he was just one lone voice, but if others speak out—a whole load of you—someone would have to listen."

"You reckon? Other growers *have* reported it. The most recent I know of was a couple of years ago and not far from here. Seaforth's are a commercial producer, much bigger than us. They *were* taken seriously. Scientists with all sorts of gadgets descended on the place and staked it out for a week."

"And?"

"Nothing. The bolters didn't show. After a week or so of kicking their heels for no return, the experts packed up their equipment and left. Rumour has it they reckoned old man Seaforth was trying it on, angling for some sort of government subsidy."

"So these things knew enough to avoid the place, then."

"Doubt it. There's no telling when the bolters will come and go. Last year they raided us three times in a week shortly before the picking season began and then left us alone for the best part of a month. When they do appear it always seems to be just after dawn but otherwise there's no apparent pattern to it."

Geoff was working himself into a real state—though whether through excitement, rage or simple after-shock was unclear. "For God's sake, it doesn't really matter about this Seaforth or what's gone on before. You *can't* justify not reporting this. It's too important. First alien contact or inter-dimensional contact, whatever it is, people have a right to know."

"Yes and no doubt they will, but not from me."

"Oh come on, what were you in a previous life, an ostrich? You can't just bury your head in the sand and hope this'll go away. You can't leave it for someone else to do the right thing simply because doing the right thing might be a little difficult."

"Watch me."

"You have a duty . . . "

"Yes, I have a duty," I interrupted, matching his growing indignation with my own. "To my son, to David; that's where my duty lies." I was almost shouted the final words

Wisely, he shut up.

I made a conscious effort to calm down. "Of course the world is going to learn about the bolters and doubtless uncover all their mysteries, but not until the world is *ready* to listen and that sure as hell isn't now. I'm not about to get myself labelled as a scammer like old Seaforth or worse, a crack-pot. Can you imagine what that would do to David? You do remember what school was like, don't you—how cruel kids can be when they get the chance?"

"Look, I can understand you feeling protective towards the boy, especially after the way Susan . . . . "

"This has nothing to do with Susan," I snapped, on the verge of really losing it and determined not to stray onto that particular subject.

At which point David came running back to the truck, his arrival effectively ending the conversation and taking the heat out of the situation. He was still far too excited to pay any attention to the mood, or to notice that Uncle Geoff said not a word on the brief drive back to the house. I noticed though, and trusted it was because Geoff had plenty to think about.

"I still don't agree with your decision to keep a lid on all of this, but I've decided to respect your wishes and keep my mouth shut for the moment," Geoff informed me as we shared a beer.

"Thank you." This hardly amounted to a solemn undertaking, but it was better than nothing.

It was Sunday. To everyone's amazement, not to mention relief, the two children had declared a temporary truce and found something to play on the computer which they could both enjoy. Rachel had gone upstairs to lie down for half an hour, complaining of a migraine. All of which left me in comparative privacy with Geoff,.

GROWING PAINS

David and I had gone out early again that morning. The bolters failed to show, which disappointed him and delighted me. There were plenty of other things that needed doing around the farm and we had little problem in filling a couple of hours with more mundane duties.

Geoff had said nothing further about yesterday's events until now and I was anxious to see where this conversation was going. Unexpectedly, he started to grin. "It's bizarre, don't you think?"

"What is?"

"First contact with aliens and it's not made by astronauts or scientists or even politicians, but by fruit farmers."

Suddenly we were both chuckling. "Score one for the little man!"

"I'll drink to that."

It was the closest I've ever felt to Geoff, that fleeting instant of camaraderie. Will he stand by his decision to stay quiet about the bolters, or will that resolve erode now that he's back in the City routine? Impossible to say; I guess only time will tell. Just give me until David has finished school and I might even start shouting about all this from the rooftops myself, but not while my son remains so vulnerable.

One thing that became clear over the course of that weekend was the growing distance between Rachel and me. Looking back, the burden of secrecy did make me unusually reticent and was certainly a contributing factor. It was nothing uncomfortable as such, but we spent the entire weekend politely skirting around each other like cordial strangers. Her obvious concerns over David only made matters worse. That was an issue I'd resolved in my own mind a long time ago and I resented her worrying, even though I could understand its cause. You see, I feel more than a little proud of my son and the way he has adjusted to life, particularly since his mother walked out on us. He has plenty of interests, willingly helps around the farm, keeps out of trouble for the most part, has plenty of friends and is doing well academically. What more could any father ask for?

He is *not* a psychopath in the making, whatever his aunt may fear. He just happens to like shooting things—an attribute that's proved more than useful under present circumstances and something which I'm convinced will not cause long term harm.

Perhaps I should have been more understanding. I think Rachel arrived genuinely wanting to get to know her only nephew a little better, but she never has been the most maternal of women, and raising Jude seems to have given her little insight into how to connect with an adolescent boy; at least, not this particular adolescent boy. She tried, but her efforts tended to come across as patronising.

She had one final go in the build-up to saying goodbye, while Geoff and I were loading the car. I came in partway through what was clearly a "what do you want to be when you grow up?" conversation.

"I bet I know what you're going to be," she said, smiling and mussing his hair in the way he particularly hates, "a soldier!"

"Nah," my beautiful son replied, giving her a huge, toothy grin, "I want to be a fruit farmer, just like my dad."

"Really?" It must have been the last thing she expected to hear.

"Sure. You get to kill more things that way."

The Assistant

As usual by the time we arrived, the underground car park was a desert of asphalt, faded white lines and inadequate lighting. Our vans were the only vehicles in sight, their headlights chasing serried stripes of short-lived shadow between the ranks of concrete pillars.

The corporate big-wigs had long since abandoned the place in favour of their homes, their fancy restaurants, clubs and bars, for the company of their wives and husbands, their boyfriends and their mistresses, leaving much-coveted parking spaces free for the likes of us: the Sanitation and Cleansing Technicians. Cleaners, if you prefer.

I always pull up in the same bay—the one with the wall plaque that reads 'Reserved', and then 'Managing Director'. As ever, that plaque was the last thing I glanced at before killing the lights.

We piled out of the vans; a human sea of grey-blue overalls, all converging on the service entrance to the building proper.

Here everyone hung back, as if unsure of themselves. In fact they were waiting for me. The name badge on my chest might say 'Assistant', but they all know who's boss. Except when Gus is around, of course—then I really am just the Assistant.

I waved at the camera; or rather, waved at the front-desk security via the camera.

"Hi, Joe," said the built-in speaker above the door.

"Hi," I replied with another wave and a grin. The system's scratchy acoustics rendered the voice anonymous and I had no idea who was on the desk that night, so chose not to risk offence by venturing a name.

GROWING PAINS

The doors hissed open and we went through, with me standing to one side, clocking everyone in as they entered—the best part of a hundred bodies in all.

'Hi, Joe' or simply 'Joe' echoed in myriad different accents, pitches and timbres as the crew funnelled through the bottleneck of the entrance. The register in my hand recorded each and every one as they passed, identifying them via the chip built into their name-badges. Within minutes the flood had become a trickle and then ceased flowing altogether. I checked the register. All those who were supposed to be here were—Kelly and Trev having both called in sick, whilst Muskrat and Yvonne were on vacation. The only other absentee was Wes, and we all knew about Wes. Out of danger now, thank God.

That was the first duty of the night taken care of. The next priority was to look in on the 22nd floor—at the time our one major concern. I shared the elevator with Mac, Josh and a timid blonde girl whose name I can never remember. I checked her badge at the time, of course, but goodness knows what it said.

Mac was in a chatty mood, whilst Josh seemed more intent on trying to catch the blonde's eye. Since the eye in question gazed unwaveringly at the floor, this was proving more difficult than Josh undoubtedly anticipated.

"Bet you're hoping for a quieter one than last night," Mac ventured.

"That's for sure."

The previous night we'd been invaded by a swarm of mini-bots, each no bigger than your little finger. Horrible things they were, looking like a cross between a woodlouse and a centipede—all jointed segments and scurrying legs. Pink had spotted them coming in through the ventilation system. We call him Pink because that's the colour of the stripe that runs front-to-back through his bleached and cropped hair. He claims to be a Post-Modern Neo-Punk. Personally I reckon he made that up, because I've never heard of any such group, clan or movement, but he swears otherwise.

Anyway, these bots had come in through the ventilation system. We've got the whole thing rigged with a mess of sensors that are supposed to be capable of picking up absolutely anything, but they managed to get around most of those.

Pink monitors the ducts and shafts—that's his bag—and if not for him we might have missed them entirely. I closed off all the vents in the building, intending to channel them towards a single meeting room on the eleventh floor. Something went wrong and instead of just the one room staying open, half the vents on the floor failed to seal. Before we knew it, they were everywhere. Fortunately there's nothing too sensitive on the 11th—just the canteen and a bunch of interview rooms—but we had a devil of a job hunting the little buggers down. Their carapaces were made of some fancy new non-metallic polymer. The only metal anywhere on them was what we presumed to be shielding around their power source, which Pink insisted should *not* be referred to as a battery for some reason. As a result they were hard to pick up on the monitors, until someone discovered that their power sources—whatever those might be—leaked a very faint energy signal. Once we pinned that down the job became much easier, but they were still tough little so-and-sos and no mistake. See one scuttling along a wall and hit it with something and it would just drop to the floor and keep on scuttling. You had to stamp on them damn hard to do any real damage. Apparently this was all due to the 'extraordinary elasticity of their polymer carapaces.' That's a direct quote from Mikey, one of the tech-heads on the team, after he'd had a chance to examine the remains of one.

The jury's still out on precisely what these bug-bots were supposed to achieve. Mikey and a few others took away some mangled remnants and partial-bots to look at in their own time in an effort to find out, but best guess is they were intended to insert something into the computer system—spy-tech, a sophisticated Trojan or maybe just a virus to wreak havoc. With their agility, resilience and the aid of whatever shielded them from most of our security systems, they very nearly made it as well. Thank God for Pink!

"Any word on Wes?" Mac asked.

Wes was the one who discovered that the bug-bots were equipped with a defence mechanism. Somehow, they were able to deliver a powerful jolt of electricity through their carapaces—metal or no metal. We avoided touching them with our bare hands after Wes went down.

I was proud of my guys' reactions. The crash team were there in a flash and got his heart going again in next to no time. Even so, it had been a horrific moment, especially when someone first turned around and told me, "He's dead."

Thankfully that pronouncement proved premature, and Wes was

GROWING PAINS

soon in hospital. I'd made a point of checking shortly before coming on shift and had been assured that he was well on the road to recovery, with no apparent sign of any brain damage.

"He's doing fine," was all I actually said.

"Glad to hear it. Wish I'd seen those little critters," Mac continued. "Heard about them, of course, but it would've been nice to have had a chance to stomp on a couple."

"You didn't miss much," I assured him.

The blonde's eyes flicked up at me as I spoke, then quickly down, without once looking in Josh's direction. I struggled not to grin at his obvious disappointment.

I was the first off, exchanging cheery farewells with the two men and even getting a brief smile from Miss Anonymous Mouse, which must have really bugged Josh.

At the 22nd the elevator opens straight into a vast open-plan office. Hilary was already there, distributing cloths, fresh bin-liners, and aerosols of polish and disinfectant to her team, while off to one side Sissy was setting up, preparing to make the routine sweep for any extraneous electronic devices.

"Off to the loo already, Joe?" Hilary called out as I passed.

"Yeah, you know me: can't keep away from the place."

She was right about my destination, of course. To be more specific, I was headed for the Ladies. A few nights previously, a greeny black mildew-like growth had been spotted in the corner behind the cistern of the end cubicle. Except that it wasn't mildew. It was an artificial construct composed of near-microscopic units that were busily self-replicating and building at an alarming rate. Once discovered, the 'infection' was easily removed and the whole area scoured and disinfected.

The next night it was back; same thing, same place. Again it was disposed of and this time we used some really heavy-duty disinfectants and cleansers, sealing off the cubicle for 'maintenance purposes' to protect the office-workers from any toxin traces the next day. None of which prevented the damned stuff from sprouting up again.

This was the fourth night and I wanted to make sure we finally had the problem licked before getting on with my regular duties.

"Any luck?" I asked Steve, the disposal team's foreman.

The look on his face was all the answer I needed.

"So what do we try now?"

He sighed. "Same cocktail of toxins we used last night, more or less—plus a few variations. The samples I took of the stuff didn't handle either electrical pulsing or a strong magnetic field too well. So we're going to be hitting it with a three pronged attack: chemical, magnetic, and electrical."

"And if that doesn't work?"

"I suppose nukes are out of the question?"

"Be serious."

"Well... Do you remember the chompers I cooked up last summer?"

For a second I didn't, but then memory kicked in to earn its keep.

"You mean those black beetle things that took care of the electric ants on 5th and 6th?"

"Yeah, they're the ones. I thought I might adapt them to develop an appetite for this muck." He nodded towards the offending cubicle.

I grinned and nodded approval. "Good move. Yes, I like the sound of that."

Steve was still looking towards the cubicle. "What do you reckon this mould is supposed to achieve?"

"Beats the hell out of me."

Infiltration of some sort, obviously, but to what purpose? In all honesty, we never even worked out how the stuff was introduced into the building. The sewers, ventilation system, human carrier, all were possibilities. Not that it was any of our concern, really—outside our remit. After all, we aren't detectives, we're just the cleaners.

No point in my hanging around, so I left Steve and his team to wage their war against the techno-mould, making a mental note to get an update later. My next stop was the 6th floor; time to check in with Jet. I knew she would have called me if anything unusual had come up, but I always like to show my face.

Speaking of faces, I never tire of looking at Jet's. Not because she's spectacularly beautiful or anything—although she might be, it's hard to tell under all the make-up. Jet is a Goth through-and-through, a fact that's obvious even when she's wearing regulation overalls. You see, Jet does not so much wear her colours on her sleeve as on her face. The make-up is spectacular, from the pale-powdered cheeks and thickened lashes to the graded eye-shadow and the layered lipstick, which shifts from deep pink outline to white at the very tip of the lips. The result is

GROWING PAINS

amazing and must take her an age to apply. I said as much to her one time, not long after she first joined us.

She looked at me in genuine surprise. "This? This is nothing—work-casual, a total compromise. You should see me when I make an effort." She meant it too.

Jet was at her usual terminal, eyes glued to the screen, not even looking up as I came in. She knew who it was.

"Anything?"

"Nope, all quiet so far. Ah . . . " Her eyes lit up.

"What is it?"

"Nothing for you to worry about; just the Ghost back to take another crack at us." Her fingers flew over the keyboard.

The Ghost was the latest in a long line of hackers who keep trying to break into the company's systems. The fact that Jet labelled him 'the Ghost' is a testament to his skill. Previous opponents included Rammer, Thick-as-Shit, the Nerd, Dopey, and Dumb-Wit—actually the 'dumb' part was my amendment, Jet had used a far less complimentary term.

Jet's hands were motionless for long seconds as she studied the screen, then she started to smile.

"I see what you're up to. Clever, very clever . . . But not clever enough." Again her fingers danced and the air reverberated with the rat-a-tat machine-gun fire of hammered keys.

"I'll leave you to it," I told her.

"Okay."

"Have fun."

"I will." Still no glance in my direction, but in fairness she *was* busy. The Ghost seemed destined for another frustrating night. I knew how good our girl was.

I continued with my rounds and it must have been an hour or so later when Pink called. Any of my supervisors can get in touch anytime they want. In theory I could spend each and every night sipping coffee with my feet up, nattering to Security at the front desk in the knowledge that I'd be contacted if anything noteworthy happened. But that's not my style. I'm more your hands-on kind of guy and would only end up fretting about what might be happening on my watch if I tried something like that. So instead, like some restless mother hen, I prowl around the building keeping an eye on things, co-ordinating resources, and providing help wherever it's needed.

"Joe," said Pink's voice in my ear, "I think you'd better get over here."
"What's up?"
"Not sure, but I don't suppose it's anything good."
Pink was on 5th, the floor below Jet. When Jet first joined us I'd put her in with Pink and his boys, but she and he had taken an instant and mutual dislike. The sniping and bitching between them became so bad that it was distracting the rest of the team and work suffered—they nearly missed an incursion that could have been disastrous—so I shifted Jet out to her current one-woman station on 6th. She seems to like it that way.

When I arrived, Pink and Simon were crowded around Del, who was busy at his work station. All three were staring at Del's screen, which was completely hidden from me courtesy of their huddle.
"What is it?"
Pink stood back and ushered me forward. "Take a look for yourself."
On the screen was a 3D simulation of... 'the kitchen'?
"Yeah. Del's been picking up a strange energy signature—very faint, almost certainly leakage rather than a deliberate signal."
This inevitably triggered memories of the previous night. Naturally the kitchen was next to the canteen, on the 11th floor. "We must have missed one of the bug-bots in yesterday's clean-up."
"Maybe."
"You don't sound convinced."
He shrugged. "Well..." After being tapped on the shoulder, Del slipped out from his chair, allowing Pink to replace him in front of the screen. "The signature's not the same. Similar, but not identical."
"Perhaps the battery—I mean power source—is damaged."
Pink made no comment. At his deft coaxing the perspective of the image started to change. We zoomed in on a work surface, squeezing between storage jars. A nebulous shape behind the jars seemed to move.
"There!" Pink exclaimed.
The image provided no detail, not even a distinct outline, just the impression of something.
"It's not a very clear picture," I grumbled.
"It's not a very clear signal."
"Has to be a bug-bot; too much of a coincidence otherwise." I sighed. "Okay, I'll go and take a look."
"Do you want some help?"

GROWING PAINS

"No; if it is just a damaged bot there's no point in pulling half the shift away from what they should be doing as we did last night... and if it's anything else, I'll let you know." I paused at the door. "I take it you can guide me to whatever it is and keep tabs on the thing if it moves around?"

"Of course."

I went to leave.

"Joe, let me come with you."

I turned around, amazed. "What's up, Pink, need some exercise?"

"No..." I'd never seen him look so uncomfortable. "But I've got a bad feeling about all of this. The bug-bots, what happened to Wes and now this, whatever it is... Something's not right, I can feel it."

I laughed and then shook my head, wondering if perhaps I'd been working him too hard. "I'll be fine. Just let me know where the damned thing is, okay?"

"Okay," but he clearly wasn't happy.

The 11th was deserted, the crew evidently having finished here and moved on. In passing I noted with approval the swept floors and glanced in at one or two of the meeting rooms—just a random sample—confirming that the bins had been emptied and the desks cleaned. Everything seemed in order.

It's funny, but the canteen, or restaurant as we're supposed to call it, is the only part of the entire building that gives me the creeps. I must have been through every room on every floor of this place a thousand times, finding each one deserted as often as not. Abandoned workstations, empty rooms that reverberate with stark knocking from the pipes and silent corridors in which every individual footstep echoes sharply—no problem. But the canteen always strikes me as spooky. This vast area, filled with row after row of empty tables and chairs... and complete stillness.

I suppose it's simply the absence of noise and bustle, of conversation and activity and the clatter of cutlery that's so much a part of canteens everywhere, but I always imagine that I can sense things here; sounds and movement—people—just beyond the reach of perception.

So I didn't linger. I looked straight ahead and walked through quickly, fixing my eyes on the swing-door that leads to the kitchen.

Even so, Pink's misgivings echoed through my mind, to be summarily dismissed. I was convinced this was nothing more than a damaged bug-bot and the previous night had taught me how to deal with the likes of them.

"Pink, you reading me?"

"Loud and clear."

"Has it moved?"

"Some, but it's still in the same general area. Don't worry; we'll lead you straight to it."

Once I'd switched on the lights, the first thing I noticed was a pail of dirty water and a mop resting against a counter. Both were in line-of-sight of the door and had obviously been overlooked by my lot when tidying up. Sloppy; I'd take care of them later and would have a word with the supervisor.

"Okay, Pink, talk to me."

"It's on that shelf to your left, the one at about head-height."

I saw the shelf he meant. "That's not where the thing was when you showed it to me, is it? Wasn't it on the work surface below?"

"Yes."

"So whatever this is, it climbs walls like a bug-bot."

"But a fair bit slower."

Which would make sense, if this were a damaged bot as suspected.

I started to walk down the aisle between ovens and work-surfaces, eyeing the shelf in question.

"You're almost there," Pink said after I'd taken a dozen or so steps.

There was still no sign of anything unusual on the shelf. I reached up and moved a large, stainless steel mixing bowl, which was the most obvious obstruction. Had I caught the suggestion of movement? If so, it was nothing that could be seen directly, but in the corner of my eye a shadow appeared to shift a fraction. I took down a second bowl... and found myself staring at the bug-bots' bigger brother. It was three or four times the size and by no means identical to the previous night's pests, but clearly came from the same lineage.

I would love to put what happened next down to my lightning-quick reflexes or a nebulous sixth sense, but in truth it was more a case of surprise and alarm mixed in equal measure. The thing was pointing its snub-nose straight towards me, and it looked for all the world like the business end of a gun. Instinctively I flinched and ducked away, just as a lance of energy stabbed out from the bot, bisecting the space my head had occupied a split-second earlier.

GROWING PAINS

I swear I felt the heat of the beam's passage, although others have suggested since that this is nothing more than an elaboration of my own imagining. Hard to say; at the time I was too busy scampering away on all fours and hauling my arse around the corner of the ovens to give the matter proper consideration.

"Joe! Are you all right? What happened?"

"The frigging thing shot at me! Some sort of energy weapon. Where is it now?"

"No idea." Pink sounded as frantic as I felt. "We've lost everything: visual, virtual—all whited-out. Ah . . . coming back on now. Five point two seconds. Remember that. If it fires at you again, I'm going to be blind for a little over five seconds."

"Thanks, I'll bear that in mind."

"I'm sending you some back-up."

"No!" I thought of what had happened to Wes and had sudden visions of people charging in and getting themselves shot. Not something I intended having to explain to Gus, let alone their families. My deepest sympathies for the loss of your son—killed in the line of duty . . . Yes, I know he was only a cleaner. It's a dangerous business. "Leave it to me."

"Don't be an idiot, Joe. What are you going to do, talk it to death? That thing's armed. You're *not!*"

"Nor is anyone else. Sending others in here will just give it a few more targets to shoot at."

"Point taken. But what *are* you going to do?"

"I'll think of something."

"Well think quickly, because it's moving along the shelf towards you. The bloody thing will have you in sight again any second now."

No sooner had Pink spoken than I saw that distinctive snub nose poke over the edge of the shelf. I scrabbled away and in doing so, again managed to avoid being singed by a hair's-breadth, as it fired for the second time, scorching the base of the wall. A detached corner of my mind registered the resultant burn-mark and recognised what a pain it would be to shift before the morning.

Five seconds was where most of my mind was focused. Pink was silent. This time even the comms seemed to have gone down. For the next five seconds I was cut off, completely on my own. Just me and the big bad Bug-bot. Did it need time to recharge between shots? *I* needed a

24

weapon, desperately. My eyes focused on the mop, across the other side of the aisle. Pausing only to pray that the thing wasn't yet ready to take another potshot at me, I flung myself over, clasped the mop and clambered to my feet.

Looking back, I think I may have shouted or roared—though goodness knows why—as I swept the makeshift weapon across the shelf, sending pans and utensils flying in all directions, clearing everything in its path. Including my automated adversary.

The five seconds must have been up around then, because suddenly Pink was yelling franticly in my ear.

"Joe, what's happen..." Which is when the bug-bot landed in the pail of water. I'm not sure whether it tried to fire again or simply shorted-out. Either way, there followed a violent flash and Pink was cut-off in mid-sentence, vanishing for another five seconds.

Breathing hard, I simply stood there—eyes fixed on the bucket. I resolved not to be so hard on the relevant supervisor after all. In fact, I might even make it a requirement to leave forgotten pails of dirty water lying around until the end of the shift.

I found that my hands were shaking. They still clasped the mop. I approached the bucket gingerly, half-expecting to see an ugly, snub nose peer over the rim, but it didn't. That flash had been the bot's final act. Reaction set in and I slumped into a sitting position, my back pressed against the units with the mop resting across my lap.

"Joe, Joe?"

I started to laugh—I couldn't help it. "Welcome back, Pink."

Some people have suggested since that the previous night's invasion of mini-bots was merely a feint, a diversion to allow their larger and nastier cousin to slip in unnoticed. I'm not so sure. Personally, I reckon this was probably an attack on two levels. The smaller bug-bots were tricky enough and numerous enough to succeed in their own right, but, in case they didn't, their larger relative sneaked in under cover of the incursion, found somewhere to hide, and powered down for twenty-four hours. Thanks to the vigilance of Pink and his crew, the tactic failed.

I waited around until the cavalry arrived, made sure that the clean-up was well in hand and that the entire 11th floor was being turned upside down and searched with a fine-toothed comb, just in case there were any more nasty surprises lying in wait, then headed off for a well-earned

GROWING PAINS

mug of coffee. Halfway to the elevator I had a better idea and gave Mac a call.

"Mac, do you still keep a bottle of single malt tucked away in that store cupboard of yours?"

"Yes," he admitted reluctantly, "for special occasions."

"I'm on my way. Believe me, this is a special occasion."

"Why, what's happened?"

"I'll fill you in over a wee dram or two."

"Deal."

I had to report what had happened, of course, which caused the Boss to come by a little earlier than usual. This is just one of three buildings that Gus has to look after. He spends most of his time over at Trans-Global. I think he fancies the Assistant there, Jocelyn: quite cute but a bit broad about the beam for my taste.

Gus is a big man and his waistline has expanded a fair bit since he got himself promoted to Senior Sanitation and Cleansing Technician a while back. Of course, that was how I came to be promoted as well because, before then, Gus had my job. He keeps kidding me by saying things like "one day you'll have this job, Joe." No thanks. It wouldn't suit me, all that flitting from place to place. I'm much happier having my own patch and just being the Assistant.

Gus dropping in a little ahead of schedule wasn't all that unusual. The pair of suits who came with him were.

Suits meant something important was afoot. They whisked in, collected the carcase of the Big Bad Bot and disappeared so rapidly that I was left wondering whether they had been there at all.

"Gus, what's going on?" I asked once we were alone.

He smiled in that chummy, jovial way of his. "Joe, Joe, not our concern. You know how it is."

I sighed. "Yeah, I know. We're just the cleaners."

He was right, of course; except that this was different. That thing had nearly killed me, and this time it was personal.

I mulled everything over long after Gus had gone. In the past few years we'd seen plenty of strange things, cunning devices and ingenious mechanisms, but nothing that had warranted the intervention of suits. Until now.

The shift was nearing its end; my people were busy packing away and getting ready to withdraw. As ever, they would leave the building minutes before the first of the office workers arrived—the eager ones, keen to impress and desperate to score points with the management.

I decided to pay Pink another visit.

There wasn't much time. Within the hour this place would be bustling. The desks would be occupied, the phone lines buzzing and the computer screens burning bright, as the 9-to-5ers went about their business, never stopping to wonder how the bins got emptied or the floor swept clean, never having an inkling as to what went on behind locked doors when they weren't about. Which is how it should be and how it's always been; so we *had* to be gone soon. But equally, I had to know.

Simon and Del looked up guiltily as I came in, reminding me of kids caught with their hands in the sweet jar. Mikey, the tech-head who had taken some of the smashed mini-bots away the previous morning, sat perched on the end of Pink's desk.

Maybe it was pure coincidence that the two members of my team who were likely to know most about these damned bots were to be found huddled together at that particular moment, but somehow I doubted it.

I told Del and Simon to knock off a few minutes early. They powered down their stations and scarpered, gratefully. Then I returned my attention to Pink and Mikey.

"Okay, you two; spill."

They exchanged a nervous glance before Pink replied. "We're not really certain of anything."

"So tell me what you're uncertain of."

"Well," Pink began, "you know I was unhappy about the energy signature we spotted coming off of the bots?"

I nodded.

"The readings were all wrong for any type of power source I know of. It was almost as if the bots were pulling energy in rather than leaking it out."

"What?"

"That fits with what I've found out from the fragments I took away with me," Mikey said, taking over. "There's nothing in *any* of them to indicate a power source, but plenty that's suggestive of power reception."

GROWING PAINS

"From where?"

There was an uncomfortable pause before Mikey took a deep breath and continued. "Okay. We all generate energy simply by moving around—friction with the components of the atmosphere we move through and with whatever surface we're travelling across..."

"Oh, come on", I cut in; "you're not suggesting *that's* how the bots are powered, are you? The energy produced must be minimal, much less than the amount that's eaten up by the movement that creates it." I remembered that much from school.

"True."

Pink chuckled and leant back in his chair, arms clasped behind his head. "This is where it gets *really* interesting."

"You've heard of quantum computers?" Mikey asked.

"Sure." This wasn't a lie. I *had* heard the term.

"Good. Then you'll know that the Chinese have built a computer containing more qubits than a lot of experts thought would ever be possible."

I nodded. *That* was the lie. I might have heard of 'quantum computers' but I had no idea what one actually was, let alone a 'qubit'.

"They've done it by combining quantum memory with cluster states. Still early days, but what they've come up with looks to be capable of outstripping even the fastest super-computer built along conventional lines."

"Cluster states...? Remind me."

Mikey raised an eyebrow, but answered anyway. "It's a kind of storage architecture, to prevent fragile entanglements from collapsing during calculations."

"Oh, right." I was left none the wiser but had no intention of admitting my ignorance a second time.

"Problem is, of course, that the known universe doesn't contain the resources to support a quantum computer operating at anything like this capacity, yet one *has* been built and it *does* seem to work."

I stared at him dumbly. Mikey was really fired up by this point, enjoying himself no end, so didn't notice my bemused expression.

"The only way that's possible is if the computer is reaching into parallel universes and drawing on resources there to supplement what it can't find in this one. Quantum computers aren't simply a new generation of computing, they're a whole new species, an evolutionary leap.

The Assistant

"I reckon our bots are working on quantum principles—reaching across and absorbing the infinitesimal amounts of energy produced by the friction of their own movement from an infinite number of realities. Insignificant in themselves, the sum of all those tiny fractions—*that's* what gives them the power to move, to produce the sort of shock that floored Wes and even to fire the energy cannon that nearly nailed you."

This may all have been way beyond me, but the implications weren't. "It would certainly explain why the two suits turned up as soon as I reported in," I agreed.

"Wouldn't it, though? We all got so carried away yesterday that we smashed the bug-bots into fragments, but that bigger bot you faced today is whole; unbattered and unstomped." Mikey grinned at me. "You may just have handed those suits the secret to a whole new form of energy."

It was now well past time for us to go, so we said our goodbyes and headed home, leaving me to wonder whether or not Mikey was right. The thing is, if I *had* handed over the key to a brand new sort of energy, then clearly somebody else already has it. And if they were willing to risk revealing the fact so casually, what else have they got?

I keep thinking of what Mikey said about the Chinese having developed this quantum computer.

Over the next few months I'm going to be watching the headlines with interest and won't be at all surprised to see an announcement about a revolutionary break-through in energy production.

The interesting thing will be to see who makes it. Not that it's any concern of *mine* who does, of course—unless, that is, they harbour further designs on this building and its installations.

After all, I'm just the cleaner; and, as it says on the badge, an assistant one at that.

WALKING THE DOG

It's funny, the sort of things that can raise a man's spirits: the clinching of that elusive deal, a cold beer when your throat is as dry as gravel, a smile from a pretty girl or the memories evoked by a few bars of a familiar song drifting from the radio; transient pleasures all. I suppose I should count myself lucky, in that I had my 'shot in the arm' every day, as soon as I arrived home from work.

This particular day had been one to forget, with rumours of redundancy and takeover sending morale at the office into free-fall. Rarely had I been more grateful to walk out of the building and head for home.

We live in a quiet cul-de-sac which cars have little reason to venture down. If the house is silent you can always hear when somebody pulls up on the drive, from the scrunching of tyres on gravel if nothing else.

So could she.

Even before stepping out of the car I heard her barking; a strong but joyful sound all her own. Suddenly the troubles of the day were forgotten, as I hurried towards the house with a ridiculous grin on my face—I couldn't help it.

Following an over hasty fumble with the keys I finally succeeded in unlocking the door, only to be accosted by an unleashed dervish: an irrepressible bundle of ginger-snap coloured fur, frantically dancing feet, beating tail and flapping ears. Sandy, my very own cocker spaniel; the dog I had always dreamed of.

"Yes, I missed you too." I crouched to pet her, receiving a waft of canine breath and a face-wash in response.

Then she was away, bounding around in frenetic circles and voicing gleeful yips, before scampering ahead of me into the kitchen, where my

GROWING PAINS

eyes flickered between the coffee percolator and the ragged scarlet lead hanging from its wall-hook. No real contest, despite the day's diet of vending machine sustenance. I'd been looking forward to this all afternoon.

Taking a quick gulp of fridge-chilled water to keep thirst at bay, I struck a compromise with my caffeine habit, promising myself a brew as soon as the walk was over.

Sandy sat impatiently as I clipped on the lead, her tail scouring the tiles with the precision of a solitary windshield wiper.

"Come on then, girl." Not that she needed any urging.

We were out the door, with Sandy tugging at the leash and ignoring my half-hearted commands to 'heel', around the corner and down the narrow lane, where she eased off a little having found things to pause and sniff at. A figure walked towards us: forty-something, fit and female—the blonde from the pink bungalow on the corner. We'd spoken before, though I never have known her name.

"Hello." A greeting more for Sandy than for me, but we shared smiles before she bent down to stroke Her Ladyship, who would happily lap-up such attention all day. Blondie was totally absorbed and so was I, thanks to the low-cut summer top the balmy weather had caused her to wear and the angle at which she chose to bend forward.

A few minutes drifted past before she straightened. We exchanged more smiles and a few banal pleasantries: "We used to have one just like this when I was a kid."

A final smile and she walked on, while we continued on our way.

Houses made way for the village green; though it tended more towards yellow and brown in this age of constant drought. Blame global warming, blame irresponsible water companies or irresponsible consumers, or just accept the world as it is and get on with life.

Here we met Arnie with Bella, his aged golden retriever. Her familiar stiff-legged gait seemed even more ponderous than usual. She eyed Sandy warily, as if intimidated by this younger, smaller dog's relentless vitality.

"How is she?" I asked.

"Oh, not so good," Arnie replied. "I took her in for a complete overhaul the other day. They say there's nothing they can do about the back leg." He fondled Bella's ear. "Not much longer for you, is there, old girl?"

"I'm sorry." What else was there to say?

Away from the green and past No. 20, where the German Shepherd barked at us through the hedge, which in turn set the terrier yapping at No. 22. We rounded the corner and I nearly bumped into the Dalmatian Lady with her two dappled companions. They sniffed at Sandy and she sniffed at them, with much ensuing circling and criss-crossing of leads. We disentangled and went our separate ways, leaving insincere smiles and tepid joviality trailing in our wake.

A left turn brought us to the garden in which Mrs. Abercrombie pottered, complete with green sunhat and an obviously aching back, which she straightened carefully at our approach. She asked after Margaret, my wife, and Jenny, my daughter, but pointedly made no reference to Sandy, who snuffled impatiently at my feet; though I did catch her looking down at one point with a pained, wistful expression.

I felt sorry for Mrs Abercrombie and all the others like her. She wasn't a dog person, you see—never had been. Mrs Abercrombie was a cat-lover through and through. She hadn't come to terms with the world as it is now, since the pandemic.

Who could have known back then? Who even suspected? We were warned constantly that it was a question of *when* rather than *if*. Flu viruses could cross species and mutate quicker than science could react, and at some point we would suffer death in plague-like proportions. If not this year then the next or the one after that...

When the much-heralded epidemic finally arrived and fatal illness spread its cloak across the face of the world, we were all too busy worrying about ourselves to notice that our pets were falling in droves. By the time we did notice, by the time anybody could spare the resources to respond, it was too late. Mutated strains were appearing daily, each more deadly than the last. Losses were not just serious, they were total. Nobody could have foreseen that, could they?

As I took my leave of Mrs. Abercrombie I found myself wondering whether she still cried. At night, when she was alone.

We headed down a narrow alleyway, bracketed by tall garden fences, which brought us full circle and home. The rich, enticing aroma of coffee on-the-brew greeted us as we stepped inside.

Jenny was there ahead of us.

"Hi, love."

GROWING PAINS

She emerged from the kitchen and glared, ignoring my greeting. "Suppose I should have guessed where you were."

Not again. "We've been over this," I replied, as I bent to unclip Sandy's lead. "You just don't understand."

"Too true I don't!" Her anger was abrupt and fierce, the fuse apparently burning long before I stepped through the door.

She pushed past me and stormed upstairs. I heard the bedroom door slam—her parting comment. There was no point in trying to bridge the chasm, not immediately.

Sandy lay on the floor, head resting on paws and tail immobile.

I crouched down to stroke her. "Are you tired, love?"

She gazed up at me with doleful eyes, not even lifting her head. Yes, she was tired. No point in overdoing it.

"Come on," I called her over to the basket. She rose and trotted across slowly, to curl up on the blanket with a grunt.

I reached behind the left ear and switched her off, then plugged her in to recharge.

Jenny would never understand what it was like for those of us old enough to remember a world before the flu, when cats and *real* dogs were still so much a part of our lives. I pitied them, my daughter and her generation, so ignorant of what they were missing.

Then again, maybe they were the lucky ones.

MORPHS

A STRIDENT RINGING WRENCHED JAKE from a dream of gore and blood—the sort of dream that he desperately hoped to escape from one day but was afraid he never would.

The phone. He let it ring, waiting for the answer phone to cut in. Jake had been offered so much financial advice in recent months, so many not-to-be-missed deals and opportunities to claim back interest on credit cards he didn't own, that he couldn't take the excitement; so he habitually monitored all incoming calls, allowing technology to absorb the saccharine spiel of the sales personnel. Given the number of such calls that were automated recordings themselves these days, it seemed wholly appropriate to let message speak to message.

Six rings and then the machine reacted, still issuing the soulless default greeting the manufacturers had preloaded, because he could never be bothered to record his own.

"Jake, it's Paula. The Leech is on his way up."

Shit, was it that time already? He unfurled from the sofa, shaking off the lingering after-effects of sleep induced lethargy. There was no point in snatching up the receiver: Paula would already have hung up and, besides, this was hardly the time for social niceties if the Leech was on the prowl.

He pulled on his jacket and scooped up keys and loose change from the side, stowing both in zip-up pockets. At the last moment he remembered to grab the map, which he forced into another pocket. Then he opened the window.

Jake stepped carefully out onto the fire escape. Paula once joked that there was something unnatural about the Leech's knack of knowing

GROWING PAINS

whenever a tenant was trying to avoid paying the rent by slipping out this way. Jake suspected that the old miser simply listened for the sound of fleeing footsteps on metal stairs. With that in mind, he determined to be as swift and silent as possible. Reaching out to grasp the outside of the railing and using that grip as a fulcrum, he half-vaulted and half-lifted himself over the edge, twisting his body to land on the platform below. It was a display of controlled strength and athleticism that would have impressed the hell out of Paula or anyone else had they been watching. He landed lightly and with little noise, knees bending to act as shock absorbers. From the resultant squat, he rose to repeat the process in one fluid movement.

Within seconds he was in the alley, landing in a crouch and pausing for a moment to listen, checking for any indication that he had been noticed. The 'whick-whick' flurry of pigeon wings—sounding like muted 'copter props—ceased as a pair of the birds returned to a window ledge, having been startled into the air by his descent. That left the inevitable background rumble of traffic, above which he could hear the persistent, angry blast of a car horn and a raucous screaming match between a rebellious child and an over-stressed mother, but nothing that related to him.

At the same time he reached out with other senses, questing, searching, but again found nothing. Everyone in the immediate vicinity was human.

Except for him, of course, and he was getting there.

He stood, took a second to adjust his jacket and then sauntered out into the street.

Jake loved Glasgow's West End. The place was becoming trendier by the day but still managed to maintain its character. He headed towards the city centre, past the university campus with its imposing gothic tower, spires thrusting jagged defiance at the heavens. He had been intending to visit the place since first arriving here but somehow never found the time. Across Gibson Street, and he peeked in through the window of *The Stravaigin*, a restaurant that epitomised this whole area for Jake: stylish, bohemian, but still proud to be Scottish and refusing to conform; ill-matched tables and assorted chairs being preferred to anything uniform. 'Stravaigin' meant 'Wanderer', which was something else Jake could relate to.

Yes, he would miss Glasgow.

Lost in thought, Jake was caught completely off-guard when something touched him. Not in any physical way; it was a sensation impossible to convey to the uninitiated, an abrasion against the psyche, a rasping inner-itch that could never be scratched. Somewhere close by, a ghost from his past had just entered the world, and wherever it trod, death would inevitably follow.

He looked around, scanning the street, scrutinising the faces of the people nearby—the tall, attractive girl whose eyes looked through rather than at him; the two women who emerged from the store opposite, and the man who scuttled recklessly across the road, pursued by a taxi's irate horn and a courier rider's flicked Vs. But he knew there was nothing to see. It wasn't that close.

Jake walked on, changing his mind about where to go. Valentino's could wait. First he needed to check on a few things. Guiltily, he realised it was more than a week since he'd last bothered to do so. Stupid. Too many things could happen in a week.

The internet café was just around the corner. Jake hated the place—it had all the ambience of a morgue on a quiet day—but it was his only means of getting regular access to the internet. Paula was always happy to let him use her snazzy state-of-the-art laptop but she wasn't always around and, anyway, he tried not to impose; particularly since it was obvious that she fancied the pants off him, which made things a little awkward. He really liked Paula as a friend, but...

Jake had a list of sites and blogs for regular checking, which were always the first places to visit. He felt a pressing urgency today, as if events were moving quickly; instinct was telling him to do the same or risk being swamped by them. Doubtless the unscratchable itch caused by the new arrival didn't help.

He skimmed the usual sites, scrolling through one after another, checking for updates and then moving on when nothing meaningful came to light. Something caught his eye and he stopped to read it more closely. A violent death, two days ago—extremely messy according to the report. It was cited as a definite morph incident by the blogger, who revelled in the name of 'Anti-Morph'. Reading through, Jake could only agree, assuming the account was accurate.

He checked some of the regular news sites for corroboration and found it: a small report of two succinct paragraphs, a minor story effectively buried within a mass of other events. A couple of other sites

GROWING PAINS

carried something similar, reporting the murder of an unidentified man, mid-thirties. None of them provided any real detail and there was no mention of excessive violence or horrific mutilation. It was just another unsolved murder in an anonymous Glasgow street—an incident duly recorded but in such a way as to imply to the casual browser that there was nothing of interest here.

The morph community was rife with conspiracy theories, some of which Jake knew to be at least partially justified. The authorities were struggling to understand what was going on. Not understanding, they were as scared as anyone else, so imposed a media blackout while prevaricating over what to do. Somebody would blow the lid on things sooner or later, but it hadn't happened yet.

A couple of the reports included a postal area. Even without checking, Jake knew it was close, but he checked anyway, taking the crumpled street map from his pocket and unfolding it, smoothing out the creases. As he'd suspected, the murder had happened almost on his doorstep—as little as a mile away.

This merely confirmed something he knew but had been trying to avoid admitting: it was time to move on. No sign of Blonde Bitch yet, but doubtless she would show up soon. He only hoped he hadn't already delayed too long.

Jake heard the gunshot when he was halfway to Valentino's, where he intended to grab a much-needed espresso. Other people must have heard it too, but he was the only one to react, so either they dismissed it as a car backfiring or they simply didn't want to know. Water follows the path of least resistance, people the course of least involvement.

That unscratchable itch became unbearable as he ran. He nearly collided with a woman in a ghastly brown coat who unexpectedly changed direction to enter a shop. In swerving to avoid her he *did* run into a portly middle-aged man with a peppered grey beard, but it was a glancing blow, shoulder to shoulder, and the man staggered but seemed likely to stay on his feet. Jake ignored the angry curses left trailing in his wake and ran on, hurtling around a corner and then into an alley behind the shops. The itch had become a roar.

Tattered bin bags, presumably ripped open by feral cats or an urban fox, spilt decomposing muck across the pavement and he nearly slipped over. Then he saw them.

It was Blonde Bitch, looking anything but her usual cool and composed self as she shuffled backwards, rapidly boxing herself into a corner. Facing her was a tall, spindly man, whose appearance marked him as one of Glasgow's innumerable homeless. Except that every sense screamed to Jake that this wasn't a man at all, at least not anymore. It was the source of his itch: a morph.

Blonde Bitch had retreated behind a cluster of tall black bins, trying to keep them between her and the morph; her final refuge. Back in the days of metal dustbins, that might have worked—they couldn't reach through metal, but plastic wouldn't even slow them down. There was no sign of the gun, assuming it was her that had fired it.

For a second he was tempted to simply walk away, to let the morph finish off the girl he had come to view with dread, suspecting her of being his nemesis, but only for a second.

Neither of them was aware of his arrival yet, too preoccupied with each other, but he knew the morph would sense him at any moment whatever the distraction. He came up behind it, approaching at a rush and thumping the thing on the side of the head as hard as he could, splitting its ear open.

It turned and let rip with an inchoate scream of pain and rage. Which was more or less the reaction Jake had hoped for. He plunged his hand into the open mouth, forcing his fingertips past the epiglottis and pushing on down through the oesophagus, thrusting more and more of his arm into the open maw. The morph tried to bite him but couldn't get much leverage with its jaws forced so wide apart. With his other hand, Jake punched the side of its head again, anything to keep it disorientated, to distract it from attempting an attack of its own.

Belatedly, the morph started to fight back, struggling to force Jake's arm away in an instinctive, desperate bid for self-preservation, but it was too late, Jake had already found its core. The creature gouged him with its nails, leaving deep bloodied troughs in his arm, but Jake hardly felt them. In his hand he grasped the nebulous, squirming centre of the monster's being and with all his strength he squeezed, feeling it bubble and flow between his fingers as he crushed it. There was a pop of imploding air and the morph was gone, leaving behind a fine mist of blood which gently settled, speckling Jake's face and arm, feeling like warm sea fret.

GROWING PAINS

"Jesus," said Blonde Bitch, sounding suitably impressed. "That was fucking amazing." American; it had never occurred to him that she might be American.

"The only way to kill them," he explained, wondering why he bothered even as he did so. He searched in his pockets for some tissue and set about wiping the spots of blood from his face. There wasn't much. "Try anything else, you might get lucky and send it back, but all you'll have done is damage it at best. Destroy the core and it's truly dead."

Looking at her, with her long, straight, platinum blonde hair and strikingly pale blue eyes, he felt a mix of conflicting, unfamiliar emotions. This was the girl whose presence haunted him. Wherever he was she eventually seemed to turn up, with her expensive outfits and her designer shades; watching him. And the morphs were never far behind. Clearly she knew about him, and knowledge was always a threat. For that, he hated her. Yet even now, with her hair an uncharacteristic mess and her clothes dishevelled, she set his heart racing in a way that confused the hell out of him.

"You're Jake Blackmore, aren't you." She wasn't asking, she was telling.

"And you're Blonde Bitch," he countered.

She snorted; a choked laugh. "Is that what you call me?"

He shrugged. "If you don't like it, give me something else to call you."

She hesitated, gazing at him as if trying to come to a decision. It was only then that it struck him: the unreachable morph-itch was muted, but it had not entirely disappeared with the morph's death.

She smiled, "Okay. Call me B."

"Which is short for?"

"Britney."

"*Britney?*"

"Yeah, I know. Blame my mom and her taste in music." Her mouth formed a peculiar expression, partway between a grimace and an embarrassed smile. "Apparently it was a choice between Britney and Christina and Mom thought Christina sounded too dull." She shrugged. "What can I say? Mom had lousy taste, but that wouldn't come as a big surprise to anyone who knew my dad."

As she spoke, she was rummaging around among the bin bags that littered the alley, emerging with a compact matt-black pistol. What little Jake knew about guns had been gleaned from reruns of old Hollywood movies, but he saw the words 'Smith & Wesson' printed on the barrel as she checked it over.

"Isn't that the same gun that Dirty Harry used?"

The girl looked across, surprised. Then she smiled, lighting up her face and stirring feelings that Jake didn't want to analyse. Being human was getting more complicated by the day.

"Yeah. His was a 44 Magnum—a real cannon. This is the 457." She held it out for him to inspect, which he did without touching. "It's a lot smaller and easier to carry around." She went back to rummaging, emerging with a black leather handbag. "I only had time for one shot before Ol' Morphy knocked it out of my hand."

She gave the bag a cursory inspection and brushed an imaginary fleck of dirt from the strap, before opening it and dropping the gun inside.

He checked his arm. The cuts were already beginning to heal. In a matter of hours they would be gone without trace. He looked up to find her regarding him with those ice-blue eyes of hers.

"That's a neat trick."

"Isn't it just." He pulled the sleeve of his jacket down quickly to cover the wounds.

"We need to talk."

Talk? He never talked, not really, not to anyone.

"Okay," he heard himself say.

He took her to Valentino's. He loved this place. A not-entirely successful cross between a family-run Italian bistro and a trendy coffee bar, it had an ambience that he found impossible to resist. Perhaps it was the slight note of discord that underscored everything here, the sense of being slightly out of kilter which made him feel so at home. He even loved the crass music. They boasted a limited rotation of CDs, of which the most frequently played was a 'soft rock' anthology comprising rock so soft that it verged on the marshmallow.

Jake chose a corner table well out of earshot of the few other patrons, and they sat down to the sounds of REO Speedwagon.

"You're not really Jake Blackmore, are you." Again there was no suggestion that this was a question. Instead the voice held a note of challenge, as if daring him to deny it.

GROWING PAINS

Jake Blackmore had been a junkie and a habitual thief, in and out of rehab and prison, stealing to support addictions that had seen him spiral ever-downward on a one-way trip. He had been approaching the inevitable oblivion that waited at the bottom of that spiral when 'Jake' took him. B's comment brought back memories which he preferred not to recall. Dreams of blood and gore, of the rending and feeding that led to short-lived relief, a blissful blunting of the drive to kill and consume: the craving that constituted existence.

"What I mean is, you're not the original," she persisted.

"I'm," he hesitated, "the improved version," he admitted at length.

"And before that you were..." She left the sentence hanging; another challenge.

"A morph." He had never said it out loud—it was an admission he had never expected to make to anyone. All of his nightmares condensed into two short words, which had spilled out in front of this woman before he could stop them.

"God, I knew it. I fucking knew it." Her face glowed with, what—excitement... horror... triumph... shock? A little of all the above, he suspected.

"How did you... I mean, you're nothing like a morph, you're human."

"Almost," he said, more casually than he felt. "And getting a fraction more so each and every day."

She shook her head, as if to deny what she was hearing, even though she must have at least suspected the truth. "How come you're so different? I mean, morphs are so...."

"Violent, savage, bestial, lacking in any sentience, living only to feed, horrifically monstrous?" he supplied.

"Well, yeah, if you want to put it that way."

"That'll do for openers, although it doesn't come close to explaining what a morph's really like, what *I* was like."

"How come you changed?"

"I came through and took Jake Blackmore."

"You killed him, you mean."

"Yes." Why was he telling her all this? Yet he continued. "And when I adopted his shape, I became, I don't know... fixed."

"How?"

He almost cut her short there, afraid to reveal too much, but he found his mouth talking despite such qualms. "He had something on him... an amulet." He had no other word for it. It rested under his shirt now, a flat metallic disc suspended around his neck on its silver chain. "An object that called to me, that meant I had to take Jake Blackmore... and once I'd done so it somehow fixed my form, and did other things too. I started to think, to feel... I started to become human."

"Wow, that's so cool. This thing, you mean it's like a magical amulet?"

He shrugged. "I've no idea."

"Haven't you tried to find out?"

"No. In case it gets damaged in the process, in case I change back. There's no way I'm ever going to let myself become..."

"A morph." She spoke the words softly as his trailed off.

He looked down and nodded. The images swam before him unbidden: the torment, the killing, the anguish and the rage, all sensed in shades of red—blood red. A place without thought or reason, where the all-consuming drive to feed was everything.

"Can I see it?"

She meant the amulet. "Maybe, one day."

"Sorry, didn't mean to push."

Really? She seemed to have been doing nothing but. Yet they talked on, with Jake explaining how the amulet had proven to be a magnet for morphs, how they were drawn to it even as he had been. If he stayed too long in any given place, morphs would start to come through in the surrounding area, getting ever closer until they zeroed in on him.

"That's how I first found you, by tracking the morph incidents through the blogs and the online community," she admitted.

He had guessed as much when she started appearing wherever he settled, and had even wondered if she might be in-league with them. He couldn't imagine how, but fear and paranoia dogged his footsteps and his dreams, and Blonde Bitch was always there.

"Why?"

"Because I'm like you," she said.

He doubted that, but she went on: "I'm not quite human."

So he heard her story, how one day she had walked into the front room of their cosy family home to find her father in the process of tearing her mother apart, literally.

GROWING PAINS

"He'd hit her before, but this was something else—a horror movie come to life in my own front room. The blood," she murmured. "It was everywhere. The carpet, the walls, even the ceiling... I never knew the human body contained so much blood."

She described how she tried to stop him, only to find herself the object of his crazed attack.

"Its hands were inside me, I mean right in-fucking-side me," she put her hand to her chest as if feeling that touch again. "Reaching for my heart." She was trembling, an aftershock of trauma. "Then my kid brother bursts in and shoots it. Didn't kill it, but made it pause. I got away. I ran; just turned and ran, leaving Bobby in there with that thing. It wasn't my pa; I could see in its eyes that that wasn't my pa anymore. The eyes burned."

The police had later found the dismembered remains of her parents and her brother. She was the only survivor.

"I was a suspect for a while. Maybe I still am—no charges have ever been brought, though." She took a shuddering breath. "I needed to understand what had happened, why my family died, so I started looking, which led me to the websites and the morphs and finally to you."

Jake had never heard of anyone surviving a morph's touch before, but he didn't doubt her for a minute. His itch was still there. Remote, almost placid and easily ignored, but still there. Somehow the attack had changed B. She was no longer fully human, just as she'd claimed. She resonated with the taint of morph.

There were more questions, mainly from her. Most he answered candidly, others with limited truth, still holding a few things back.

"Why do you always call yourself Jake, even though you change your surname from place to place?" she asked at one point.

"I'm still getting used to being human, still learning what that means. I need that sense of identity, so the name's important. But so is not being found. Therefore I compromise; change one name but keep Jake, which is the bit I think of as 'me' in any case. Maybe I'll get adventurous next time and call myself Jack."

She laughed. "You're getting a handle on that elusive human trait 'humour', at least."

Then she asked, "Do you still hunger for human blood and organs?"

"No," he lied. *Only in my dreams.*

"Where did you learn to handle a gun?" he asked in turn.

She shrugged, "I was raised in the States." It was a partial answer, he could sense that. Not a lie, but a glib response that papered over the thousand details she clearly preferred not to discuss. He wondered whether she sensed anything similar in his own answers.

"How do you think the original Jake got hold of the amulet?"

"He stole it."

She looked at him sharply, as if he had revealed something vital. "You absorb memories then, do you, when you take somebody?"

"No." He shook his head. "Nothing that specific. It's the sort of thing Jake would do though, and how else did he come to have it?"

He had his own questions about the amulet, things he kept to himself, like why did the original Jake keep hold of it instead of selling it on? Was it through some sentimental attachment, or was it more than that? Did the amulet affect humans—perhaps destabilising the wearer in an inverse to the way it affected morphs? Was Jake's disintegration due solely to the drugs, or had the amulet played a part? He knew so little about the thing, except that it was powerful and, for him personally, vital.

All he actually said was, "Maybe if I can find out who he stole it from in the first place, I can find some answers—things like who I am, what I am."

"Is that what you're doing—looking for the real owner?"

"I wish. Right now I'm just concentrating on staying alive, on keeping one step ahead. I need to get a handle on that before I can do anything else." He looked at her, troubled by his own candidness and hoping it wasn't a mistake to talk so freely. In a few moments he had said more to her than he'd ever told anyone.

They headed back to his place. Afterwards, he could never remember who first suggested it, they simply went.

He stopped after a few paces, taking out and lighting one of his precious supply of roll-ups, prepared earlier that day.

"Those things'll kill you in the end," she said.

"Not me they won't."

He knew something was wrong the instant they stepped through the street door. If he hadn't been so wrapped up in B he would surely have sensed it earlier. The place reeked of morph. She could sense it too. Her hand strayed towards her bag and the pistol it contained.

GROWING PAINS

His gaze darted around the entrance hall, looking for something out of place and he saw it almost immediately. The door to Paula's apartment was open. Not wide open, but enough; she was a stickler for keeping it locked. Even so, he knocked, hoping against hope, but there was no reply. Jake led the way inside, with a growing sense of foreboding, and stepped into a scene that both of them remembered from their nightmares.

The residue of Paula's torso lay in the centre of the room—facedown, thank God. Blood was everywhere. Britney gagged and fled to the loo. Jake simply stood there, looking at a red splatter-trail that climbed and fell across one wall like some surrealist's rendering of a roller coaster. Morphs went after the vital organs and the blood, but they were hardly efficient feeders. They entered a body and literally tore it apart from the inside. He could picture in his mind's eye the rending wound that had caused that flat-looped trail.

He looked back at what remained of Paula's body—a friend in a life that had known all too few of those. He had done this. His presence had drawn the morph here.

Some friend.

His morph-itch had been going crazy ever since they entered the building but even so, he should have had more sense than to stand with his back to the door and he should have paid more attention to that inner alarm.

As it was, the first thing he knew was agony.

A searing pain emanated from just below his left shoulder blade, as if something were peealing the skin away and probing beneath. He twisted his head around to find himself staring into a parody of the Leech's face. Mouth contorted in a snarl that revealed yellowed teeth and lead-grey fillings, spittle dribbling down a stubbled chin and eyes that burned with insanity and hunger. He tried to pull free, but still the morph bored into him, reaching towards his heart. The pain, which was too intense to even think of fighting back, forced him to his knees; and still it intensified.

A gun barked, then again. Instant relief as the morph staggered back, pulling out of him. Jake felt rage welling up inside, threatening to engulf him—a pale shadow of what it was to be morph, but the closest he had come to such a thing in a long while.

B stood in the bathroom doorway, gun levelled at the creature that wore the Leech's face, which had turned its attention to her. She fired again, striking it in the shoulder and forcing the thing back a few grudging steps, but only temporarily. Jake leapt to his feet and attacked, not bothering with anything as subtle as the mouth this time but striking directly at the thing's chest, rage driving his hand to burrow morph-like into the body until he reached the core. Without hesitation he squeezed and the thing imploded, vanishing immediately.

A few seconds, that was all it had taken: a few seconds in which he had very nearly died.

"Are you okay?" B was in front of him, hand on his shoulder, which still smarted but was recovering. It was the first time she had touched him.

"Yes, I'm fine. Thanks," both for asking and for saving his life. He looked around, gathering his wits, knowing that time was against them. More morphs, the police, other tenants, someone was bound to turn up at any minute. "Have you touched anything?"

She thought for a moment. "The bathroom door, faucets, basin—I think that's about it."

"Wipe them. Then we need to get away from here, fast."

"I've got a car, it's a Mercedes sports."

Of course it was. "That'll do. Maybe it should have been Rich Bitch rather than Blonde Bitch."

She dropped her eyes. "Something like that. The insurance ... my parents."

There was nothing he could think to say. She met his eyes again, smiling to show that it was okay. "So where are we headed?"

"I don't know. Where do you live?"

"Around. I've got a place, but it's rented out."

"South, then," he said for no particular reason. "York. I've always fancied visiting York."

"Okay, York it is."

Jake watched as she bent to wipe the bathroom door handle, her back to him and her skin-tight trousers pulled even tauter by the act. There was a connection here, unlike anything he had experienced before. He felt uncomfortable at the prospect of travelling with someone else—sharing was a skill he had never needed to learn—and still felt confused by his reaction to this enigmatic woman; uncertain that he could trust his own decisions around her. Would he really be able to handle this?

GROWING PAINS

"Enjoying the view?"

He averted his eyes guiltily as she straightened, annoyed at himself and embarrassed. But when he looked back again, she was smiling. "Don't worry, a girl likes to be looked at . . . sometimes."

He'd cope, he decided.

Peeling an Onion

GIL HAD NOTHING AGAINST JOB INTERVIEWS as such; he just hated the psychological games they usually entailed.

This particular interview mattered. Failing it was not an option. Having fallen foul of Cambridge traffic in the past, he allowed for possible delays and arrived early, which enabled him to enjoy a leisurely latte in a coffee bar opposite before presenting himself at the given address.

The slim, trim and magazine-smile secretary ushered him to a small partitioned reception area by her desk. Bright red two-seater sofa units, doubtless chosen carelessly from an office furniture catalogue, sandwiched a square glass-top table to form a compact corner set. Gil accepted the offer of a coffee without thinking; a decision he regretted as soon as he sampled the scalding and bitter brew. The mug sat, quarter-drained, on the table beside him.

He had done his homework, of course. He knew that five years ago the respected Genetic Designs U.K. had undergone a facelift, rebranding itself as the jazzier Gene Genies, reputedly on the advice of a marketing agency following a multi-million euro consultation. It was argued that, with the company now breaking into the lucrative Japanese, Swiss and Indian markets, potential clients might consider any business calling itself 'U.K.' to be too provincial.

Whatever the truth in that, since the rebranding the company had gone from strength to strength and was now established at the very forefront of genetics research and design. In part, that was why Gil was here, why he chose to subject himself to the interview process despite his distaste.

GROWING PAINS

Fourteen minutes after the scheduled time, the secretary informed him that Mr. Deerham would see him now. Fourteen minutes—just enough of a wait to impress upon him what an important and busy man the interviewer was, just enough time to allow him to dwell upon and magnify any nervousness he might feel... on the other hand, perhaps the previous appointment had simply overrun by a few minutes.

In contrast to the modern efficiency of the open plan outer office, Deerham's inner sanctum proved wholly traditional; its heavy, dark wood desk and well-upholstered chairs seeming a trifle archaic and almost quaint by comparison. Deerham himself was short, podgy and balding, and he wore a tie that managed to clash with the weave of his suit. He greeted Gil with a firm but slightly sweaty handshake, before guiding him to a chair. He then surprised Gil by introducing himself as the senior project manager. Not personnel? Not an interview specialist?

"I insist on interviewing geneticist candidates myself," Deerham explained obligingly. "It's important we choose the right person, someone who's going to really mesh with the team we've built here." He entwined his fingers firmly to emphasise the point.

"Yes, of course." Gil did his best to smile and look impressed at the same time.

As the interview progressed he grew increasingly confident. There were no mind games being played here, no psychological subtexts underpinning Deerham's questions. The usual "what special qualities do you have to offer?" and "why should we choose you in particular from all the applicants clamouring for this position?" and the blunter "why are you applying for this job?" were all presented and smoothly dealt with. Gil began to relax.

Then: "I see you worked with Dr. Fleishman."

That focused Gil's attention, "Yes, for eighteen months."

"A great man, great man," Deerham said, nodding sagely.

A puffed-up buffoon living off a reputation built when the field was in its infancy, before keener, more original thinkers had entered the picture. Gil hid the thought behind a polite smile.

To his amazement, Deerham did much of the talking in the latter stages of the 'interview'. Gil felt he had the man's measure now—a generalist; someone with a broad basic knowledge of most aspects of genetics, who could grasp the concepts and follow the progress of a dozen different projects, whilst lacking the vision and ability to further or complete any of them. Capable rather than dynamic. In short, the perfect man to oversee and co-ordinate the varied programs said to be ongoing behind closed doors here at Gene Genies.

"Of course, genetics had already come on in leaps and bounds by the turn of the century." Deerham was in full flow now. "It was possible even then to tell whether a person would be susceptible to a stroke or heart disease, whether they were likely to have blue-eyed or brown-eyed children..." For fuck sake. Gil worked to keep his smile animated and to nod in the appropriate places—this was ground covered by first year students. "... but in the last decade there's been a revolution in the field. One we're at the forefront of; and we're going to stay there. Do you know why?"

Good grief. "People, I would imagine," Gil replied smoothly. "You employ the best and get the best from them."

"Precisely," Deerham said with delight, making him feel like a schoolboy who had just given the correct answer in front of class. "That's why I conduct these interviews personally; to ensure I choose the best, so that they can produce their best—for us, for themselves... and for each other."

After the interview had concluded, Alex Deerham took time to bask for a few moments in the warm glow of satisfaction. He felt very pleased with himself. It was so rewarding when someone like that walked in through the door. He had no doubt that Gil Lambert was the right man for the job. His qualifications were impeccable and he came highly recommended. In fact, to have achieved all that he had at such a young age was remarkable. But, on top of that, Deerham had found him a very personable lad. He liked him. Yes, Lambert would fit in extremely well.

Gil started at Gene Genies two weeks later.

One thing that impressed him straight away was that everyone seemed to mix and socialise freely, irrespective of what project they were working on. However, he soon realised there was a definite hierarchy amongst the research teams, even though it was never spoken about and caused surprisingly little tension. In his mind's eye he came to look upon Gene Genies as an onion, the teams representing the layers

GROWING PAINS

that had to be peeled away in order to reach the centre, the lure that had brought him here.

The first two weeks were set aside for him to acclimatise, to find his feet. So he worked briefly with Paul Thompson's team, the outer layer of the onion, who were doing several routine investigations. His workmates seemed to accept him readily enough but he made no real friends—all parties knew he was destined for greater things and would soon be moving on.

Sure enough, at the end of two weeks he was reassigned to the second layer of the onion, Sarah Cohen's team. Here he worked with Keith Howell, the man he had been brought in to replace. Howell had been headhunted for a position with a rival company in Canada. There seemed no acrimony over his departure either from the other team members or from his current employer. Again Gil settled in quickly and was well liked by his team mates. At Howell's leaving party it became apparent that one of them, Kerry Malone—a pretty young redhead—particularly liked him, which was a situation that would have to be watched. She was a nice girl: vivacious, witty and intelligent... He was more than a little tempted, but there was too much at stake. He had no intention of becoming involved in a relationship at work, with all the distractions and tensions that could lead to. Being seen as an unsettling influence was definitely not part of his game plan. He succeeded in deflecting her attentions without causing any apparent offence.

Cohen's team were working on a project involving a fresh approach to Huntington's disease. In actual fact, their undertaking was an offshoot of the main project, which was based at Gene Genies' London centre. Most of the hard work had been done by the time Gil came on board but, perhaps because he brought with him a fresh perspective, he was able to spot a wrinkle that enabled them to wrap things up a couple of days early. Which did him no harm.

Immediately after the results were submitted, Gil was seconded onto Lee Weston's team, who had just been given a Department of Health contract and would need a few extra pairs of hands to ensure they hit deadline.

The move came as no surprise to anyone. Another layer peeled away.

So passed more than a year, with Gil steadily burrowing deeper into the fabric of the company.

Then, one damp November morning, his patience and effort were rewarded. He found himself invited to Deerham's office.

This was the first time he had been there since the job interview. It had changed little in the interim. The block where Deerham spent much of his time represented the public face of Gene Genies and was in a separate building to the labs. To Gil, immersed for so long in the environment of research, it was like stepping back into another world.

Deerham greeted him warmly, enthusing about Gil's work and explaining how his progress had been watched with "interest and approval". Then came the moment Gil had been working towards: the invitation to join Edwards' team—the elite, the one team that went against the usual pattern at Gene Genies. Its members kept themselves to themselves, were tight-lipped about their work and tended to socialise within their own team—not exclusively, but almost so. This despite the fact that many of them had worked their way up through the other teams in a similar way to Gil.

There was an unspoken assumption that their work was sensitive enough to warrant such insular behaviour. Hence they had been landed with the tag *the elite*—part mocking, part grudging respect.

"It's this loyalty thing they have to sign," Greg, an Australian with whom Gil had developed a peripheral friendship, once explained. "They have to swear not to discuss their work with anyone, even the rest of us, on pain of death, prosecution and permanent torment in the afterlife; not necessarily in that order."

"Doesn't that bother everyone else? I mean, with them acting so aloof?"

"Nah. They don't party, never chill ... why should that bother us? It's their problem, their choice."

Which was entirely true. It *was* their choice and there had to be a reason why they chose to cut themselves off from friends and colleagues. Gil had just been given the opportunity to find out what that reason was. He had also been given the infamous 'loyalty contract'—for loyalty read secrecy.

Gil had custom-designed legal software loaded onto his pocket comp.—a gift from an old girlfriend with a talent for such things. With Deerham's permission he ran the loyalty contract through the program. It produced a summary of salient points, flashing up areas of specific concern in red—restrictive clause ... restriction of practice ... prohib-

GROWING PAINS

ited... legal recourse... prosecution—nothing unexpected, although the restrictions on future work were particularly harsh. Under normal circumstances he would have considered them unreasonable and refused to sign. However, the current circumstances were anything but normal.

Satisfied, he turned his attention to the LCD touchscreen built into Deerham's desk and the contract currently displayed upon it. A flashing amber box invited him to donate a thumbprint. After the briefest hesitation he accepted the invite, with Deerham pressing his own flesh to screen just underneath, on behalf of the company.

"Congratulations!" It occurred to Gil that this was a warmer welcome than he had received when first joining. "I know you've met Dr. Edwards, but let me take you down so that he can formally introduce you to the team."

Nick Edwards was a very intense man. Gil had met him several times over the past year, usually at formal parties and company events. On each occasion he had been impressed both by the man's intellect and by the control he exerted over that intellect. Very focused. Not someone to underestimate.

His office was far more Spartan than Deerham's—an afterthought added on to the research lab; somewhere to deal with bureaucracy and admin without its encroaching on matters of real importance.

Gil listened intently as Edwards described the work his team were engaged in.

"Two years ago we initiated our own research program..."

"Discretely, of course," Deerham cut in. "Wouldn't want the competition catching on." He finished the comment with a hearty chuckle.

Edwards' response was a thin smile, "Quite." It was clear he had little time for the senior project manager. "The details are on file. You can review them this afternoon; it'll help bring you up to speed. Suffice to say, the results supported our suspicions.

"Latent telepathy is part of our genetic makeup and has probably been a crucial factor in human development throughout history."

He said it simply, without drama, in a voice that could have been used to deliver any accepted truism—he might just as easily have announced that if you boil water in standard conditions it turns to steam.

"Telepathy," Gil clarified. "You're studying telepathy."

"The genetic agency of *latent* human telepathy," Edwards corrected.

Gil allowed himself a slight shake of his head as he absorbed the information.

"Incredible, isn't it?" Deerham enthused, clearly missing the flash of disdain that crossed Edwards' face at the comment.

"In truth, I hate the term 'telepathy'," Edwards continued. "It's evocative and inaccurate, but every other phrase we've coined to date has been unwieldy and, quite frankly, ludicrous. So for the moment, we're stuck with 'telepathy'.

"However, allow me to explain exactly what we're talking about here and why I stressed the word latent." This was coming across like a prepared speech, Gil realised. Was that because Edwards had used the patter for previous new team members? Or was he rehearsing for a future awards ceremony?

"We're not talking about people sitting across the room and having a conversation with their minds, or being able to tell which symbol is displayed on a playing card—it's far more subtle than that, which is the main reason this has escaped notice for so long. We are talking about influence... and subconscious influence at that.

"There are certain individuals, we refer to them as dominants, who possess the ability to influence the decisions and thoughts of those around them. In practical terms, they actually instigate thoughts for other people, with the whole process carried out at a subconscious level, both for the dominant and the subject.

"Allow me to give you an example: say, a dominant calls round to see a friend. As the friend answers the door, our dominant is thinking 'God, I hope he offers me a drink, I'm gasping'. As the door opens, our dominant says no more than 'hello', to which the friend responds with, 'Hi, come on in. Can I get you a drink?' An apparently normal conversation sequence, except that both sides of the conversation were actually triggered by one party—the dominant. It can be a thousand different things, big or small—'he's gorgeous, I hope he talks to me'... 'Go on, take me to the game instead of him'... 'Hope she likes me, she could give my career a real boost'... 'I'd love some of those crisps'... 'Give me a hint of the answer'... 'Why don't you go shopping this morning? I could use a lift'—all thoughts that might flash through a dominant's mind and would be responded to by the given subject. A dominant uses this ability constantly in everyday life without giving a second's thought

GROWING PAINS

as to how often his or her desires are responded to. To them it's as natural and instinctive as breathing.

"We have evidence that this has been going on for generations, possibly even back into prehistory. It seems likely that dominants have always been among us."

"And no one's ever suspected any of this before?" Gil said swiftly as Edwards paused for breath.

"No. Well... not specifically. Who knows? Maybe the odd dominant has been burned as a witch, revered as a wise man or worshipped as a demigod." He waved a hand dismissively. "I'm sure that if we studied history closely enough, the presence of dominants could explain all manner of events, but the true nature of the ability has remained undiscovered. Three reasons;" he started counting points off on his fingers. "One: as I've mentioned, the ability is extremely subtle and not even recognised by the dominants themselves. Two: dominants are extremely rare—one in a hundred thousand or perhaps one in a million—no way we can find out for certain without being too obvious about it, but it's definitely in that order of magnitude. Three: as I said, dominants have been around for a long, long time. I believe they go back to an age when humans were comparatively few in number. Now we've already established the subtlety of the process. It seems likely that the subjects—the rest of us—have inherited from our ancestors an acceptance of the dominants' touch, that in effect, we are all preprogrammed for ignorance. Evolution has given us a genetic blind spot that leaves us incapable of recognising the dominant's thoughts as an intrusion."

Edwards finished triumphantly, watching Gil for a reaction. For his part, Gil's respect for the man had grown; imagination to match his intelligence—a very rare combination.

For Gene Genies to be supporting and obviously encouraging this project, it must all have been thoroughly researched and documented. "I'll be able to see your findings to date?" he ventured.

"Of course."

"How does it work? I mean, have you identified the mechanism by which the dominant's thoughts are transmitted?"

"Good." Edwards gave an approving nod. Clearly that was the right question. "Yes we have. We're even close to identifying the gene responsible for passing on the ability. We know it's hidden somewhere in the introns—the 90% of human DNA that doesn't code for protein synthesis and was originally dismissed as junk. Most of it is junk, of course, but even after you've discounted the repeats and all those sequences that are residual coding from invading viruses, there's still a lot of DNA we haven't fully accounted for... but you were asking about the mechanism. As you know, the brain transmits instructions to the body via electrical impulses which are carried by the nerves. The dominant's influence works on a similar level, in a similar fashion. Normally, the brain's instructions are limited by the extent of the nervous system, which is contained within the body, but the dominant has access to an additional system, which carries the impulses beyond the physical boundary of the skin.

"We have been studying three individuals, all identified as dominants..."

"I thought you said they're incredibly rare," Gil cut in.

"Rare as rocking horse shit," Edwards confirmed, his candidness surprising Gil. "But we knew what we were looking for. People with charisma, those who are said to have 'the gift of the gab', who can 'sell ice to the Eskimos', who can 'charm the pants off' of any man or woman they fancy... in effect, anyone who has a reputation for being unusually charming, persuasive or lucky. Of those, only a tiny proportion are of interest to us—dominants are invariably successful people, but not every successful person is a dominant—so we were still looking for a needle in a haystack, but we had at least managed to make it a much smaller haystack. Even then it took us years and to date we've only found one in this country."

"But you succeeded in finding three, whom you've been studying," Gil said, impatient to steer the conversation back on-topic.

"Quite. What do you know about the Kirlian aura?"

"Kirlian aura?" Gil paused to draw a breath. "Not much. Discovered last century by a Russian scientist, whose name it bears... but I thought it had been dismissed long ago as a meaningless manifestation of electric discharge, pressure, temperature etc., or was it as an unimportant by-product of metabolism? Something of the sort."

"*Rediscovered* by Semyon and Valentina Kirlian in 1939, to be more accurate—the effect had been observed and commented on before. But you're right, it has been dismissed, perhaps a little too readily. You see, we've found that when a dominant exercises his subconscious ability,

GROWING PAINS

his or her Kirlian field expands remarkably. In effect it reaches out to brush against the Kirlian aura of the subject. As you just mentioned, the field is partly electrical in nature and we now know that the aura isn't simply a redundant by-product, that it does serve a purpose. It enables a dominant to transmit mental commands to a subject in much the same way that we all fire commands throughout our own bodies. A dominant uses Kirlian auras as a secondary nervous system, to influence, or perhaps command, the people around him."

Gil sat without commenting, outwardly appearing stunned by what he had just heard; inwardly struggling to contain the excitement that seethed within him.

That night he returned home exhausted but still elated. The whispered hints and nebulous rumours that first drew him to Gene Genies had proven true. Fragments were all he had heard; just enough to attract his interest and arouse his curiosity, though he doubted whether anyone else could have sieved from such scraps the possibilities he instinctively saw.

All the work and effort of the last year had borne fruit—the final layer of the onion had now been peeled away.

Relaxing in his favourite chair, he reviewed the day's events, focusing on an apparent triviality which had crystallised his sense of triumph. It was nothing really, just a snatch of conversation shared with Deerham on the way back from the meeting with Edwards.

It amused Gil to realise that Deerham, this consummate pen pusher, the definitive grey man, was obviously fully caught up in the excitement of this apparently far-fetched project. Deerham had said, in his excited way, "Can you imagine what it would be like to have conscious control over an ability like that?"

Oh yes, Gil allowed himself a smile, *I can imagine that very easily. Why do you think you gave me this job in the first place?*

"The only thing you'd ever have to worry about would be potential competition from other dominants."

Not really. Not when you can put yourself in the perfect position to monitor and control even that . . .

The future looked bright—always had from Gil's perspective, but now that he had discovered Gene Genies it looked brighter still.

A Question of Timing

JERRY IS UNIQUE. At least, to the best of my knowledge he is.

Unfortunately, that makes him fucking hard to explain and equally difficult to describe. But I'll try.

You see, I never had an imaginary friend as a child. No invisible playmate or giant rabbit, none of that crap. I know some kids do and that's fine, but my mind simply wasn't wired that way.

Jerry didn't appear until I was in my late teens, and he *wasn't* imaginary, just imperceptible to everyone else.

We first met at my brother's funeral. Eighteen months older than me, Paul had already progressed to university: Nottingham, to be precise. I think that made it all the more difficult for everyone—the fact that he died so far away from home, in a place that none of us had ever seen and couldn't even picture. Alone, in some insignificant residential street during the early hours of one Sunday morning, on his way back from a party. Apparently he was on his own and relying on shanks' pony after having rowed with his girlfriend. Less than sober, certainly, at least to judge by the alcohol levels in his blood. Maybe what happened was his fault, but that hardly explained the vehicle's failure to stop.

From second term student to anonymous statistic in one transient hit-and-run instant.

The police never caught the driver.

His death affected us all in different ways. Dad simply became more reticent, more distant, as if by shutting the rest of us out he could shut off the pain, while Mum took it especially hard and had real problems coping. She held everything together somehow, 'for the family', but I'm

GROWING PAINS

not sure she ever fully recovered. I'd hear her crying at odd moments for years afterwards, when she thought no one else was about. Paul had always been her favourite,

To me, my brother's death didn't seem real. He had been so irrepressibly vital, such a solid and dependable, ever-present element of life, that I kept expecting him to wander into the room at any moment as if nothing had happened and flop into the chair by the radiator as he always used to. *His* chair—the one with the shiny worn patch on the right arm where he habitually rested his elbow. None of us ever sat in that chair afterwards, except visitors, and whenever one did, I always vaguely resented them and wondered whether Mum did too, behind her paper-thin smile and vapid conversation.

It wasn't fair, Paul's death. The timing was all wrong. The whole of his life was still in front of him. This wasn't how things were supposed to go.

The funeral itself passed in a blur. I couldn't have said afterwards what the minister looked like, which hymns were sung, or what had been said in Paul's memory. My only clear recollection was of talking to Jerry, though even the details of that conversation remain a little hazy.

It was back at our house, at the 'reception'—if that's the right word in the context of a funeral. If we were Irish it would have been a 'wake', but there was no sense of celebration here, just a general numbness.

He was dressed in black, of course—a double-breasted suit—and I remember thinking that his hair was virtually the same colour as the suit. No tie, but his top buttons were undone in a way that suggested one had recently been removed, as if he'd dutifully suffered such stricture during the service but had wrenched it off immediately afterwards. I didn't recall seeing him at the service itself, but then I didn't recall seeing anything.

He seemed to know Paul, though, and I found myself talking to him, recollecting all the things I would miss about my brother and in the process laying bare the hurt in a way that I never would have with anybody else, not even my parents. Especially not my parents. His being a stranger made such candidness easier, somehow.

It's funny, but beyond his name I didn't think to ask who he was or how he knew my brother. We were about the same age and I just assumed he was one of Paul's friends from uni, a few of whom had come down for the funeral.

A QUESTION OF TIMING

After he'd gone I spoke to a couple of them and asked about Jerry. Nobody admitted to knowing him and no one could recall seeing the individual I tried to describe.

In the months that followed I started bumping into him at odd, infrequent moments. When I was sitting in a Café Nero killing time over a latté, or in a pub waiting for friends, he would just pop up, looking a little sheepish, shoulders slouched slightly and hands sunk up to the knuckles in the pockets of his tight jeans. Never when I was in company, and he'd always be gone by the time anybody else showed up.

Not once did I consider offering him my mobile number, nor did he try to give me his—it wasn't that kind of a friendship, it was more . . . spontaneous; haphazard even.

Apart from the funeral, the only time Jerry ever appeared when there were others about who might remember him was the final time, when I suppose he didn't have much choice.

It was my fault, inevitably. I'd never seen the sea like that before: so wild, so fierce, so wanton. We were in Devon, a whole gang of us. I was at uni myself by then, and this was our summer reunion—me and the gang. We didn't all travel down together but arrived in dribs and drabs, our numbers swelling as the weekend established itself. There was this festival, a two day event; it was summer on the coast and everything was going to be wonderful. We weren't going home again when the music finished, oh no. We were here to holiday—sunshine, picnics, sex and wine, the coast to explore, beaches to lie on, Dartmoor to traipse around and real ale to sup in *real* English pubs that were just waiting to be stumbled upon in the most unexpected places. Maybe even a bit of surfing, if we were lucky. What could be better? What could possibly go wrong?

Well, the English weather for one. It poured down. High winds and driving rain turned the field where the festival was supposed to be staged into a quagmire. But that was okay; we'd survived Glastonbury, so this was nothing. Then the canopy protecting the main stage blew down and the festival was declared dead in the water, so to speak.

"Summer storm," a local told us phlegmatically that first night as a few of us gathered in a nearby pub and tried to dry ourselves in front of the log fire, lit especially for us by the sympathetic landlord.

The next day, we started to separate, the gang fragmenting into little groups and couples as we drifted off to do different things, with a firm commitment to meet up again that evening.

GROWING PAINS

I had lecherous designs on Shawna, who might not have been a head-turning beauty as such, but she possessed a certain unquantifiable something. She was confident and self-opinionated, fresh faced, with an unruly mass of sandy-blonde hair and curves in all the places where women used to be proud of having curves before size zero became the yardstick. For some reason, I convinced myself that in the relaxed atmosphere of a festival she would finally succumb, would be dazzled by my wit and seduced by my sophistication and charm.

Unfortunately, it was obvious even this early in the holiday that Aaron was the one she fancied, not me. This particular day the three of us ended up going off in my car. I'm not sure why, whether I just wanted to be awkward, to get in the way and obstruct their fun, or if I still stubbornly clung to the hope of turning her head even while suspecting I was destined to play gooseberry.

We took sanctuary in a miserable café in some anonymous seaside town, because there was little else to do. The place was virtually deserted, most holidaymakers having the good sense to stay indoors and wait out the storm, so we were able to claim a table at the front, by the large plate-glass window, and stare out at the weather and the world. The only things between us and the sea were the road, a wide pavement that the local council probably called the promenade, and an ornate metal balustrade.

Through the driving rain we watched the tips of the very highest waves top the wall and cascade onto the promenade, as a disgruntled sea flung itself against the land.

"Don't worry, it won't come over; not enough to worry about at any rate," the scrunch-faced man with the sideburns said as he served us our coffees. "Tide's too low."

His accent was pure north London, on the Essex side, rather than West Country, and we hadn't been worried until he suggested the possibility.

Initially all three of us were in good spirits, joking about the weather and our misfortune, but that soon changed and while the coffees steadily drained away I began to feel increasingly marginalised, as Shawna and Aaron concentrated on each other and their casual conversation slipped seamlessly into flirting.

I responded to this by sulking; not that either of them noticed, and then by uttering petulant and vitriolic comments whenever one of

A QUESTION OF TIMING

them *did* deign to remember my existence. My only reward was a disapproving frown from Shawna and a self-satisfied smirk from Aaron.

Flirting never has been my idea of a spectator sport. Unwilling to sit there and suffer any more, I pushed myself to my feet and stalked towards the door.

"Where are you off to?" Shawna wanted to know.

"Thought I'd take a closer look at the sea,"

"Don't be stupid."

Aaron's 'let him go, he's only after a bit of attention', followed me through the door. Any further comment he might have made was swallowed by the howling wind and the drum of rain against my hood, which was pulled up hastily as I stepped outside.

Part of me half-hoped that Shawna might follow me, but by the time I'd crossed a road devoid of traffic and reached the promenade it was clear she wasn't going to. By then, I was even admitting to myself that she'd have to be an idiot to do so. As things stood, the only idiot in sight was me, for being out here in the first place. Stubbornness was all that kept me striding towards the sea wall, shoulders hunched forward against the elements, sodden trousers clinging to my legs with every miserable step.

My hands were soon brushing brittle flakes of paint from the iron balustrade that marked the edge of the promenade, as they sought a smoother grip.

In this mood the ocean was magnificent and impossible not to admire, even managing to breach the cocoon of self-pity I'd wrapped around myself. For several minutes I just stood there, watching the relentless waves and feeling the sea's fret mingle with the rain against my face. Then I wanted a closer look, wanted to see the moment the breakers crashed against the wall. So I leant out, pushing against the railing, straining for a better view . . . which is when the upper rail came loose and fell away. My weight already committed forward, I began to topple, unable to regain my balance as the broiling waves rushed towards me.

It wasn't my life that flashed before me in the split second that followed but rather a vision of what was to come. I knew I was about to die, that nothing I could do would make a difference—any struggle of mine was insignificant in the face of such elemental power. As soon as I hit the water I would be dragged under, then hurled against the sea wall, rendered unconscious by that first impact if it didn't kill me. The only question was whether I would drown before my frail skeleton and skull were shattered by constant battering against the unforgiving stone.

Suddenly I wasn't falling anymore, but instead hung motionless for a surreal instant above the churning water. Then understanding penetrated my thoughts: somebody had caught me. Legs and body thumped against the harbour wall as my fall was interrupted.

"Grab my hand!" A man's voice, made hoarse by the need to outshout the elements.

I twisted around and scrabbled at the stonework, as my saviour adjusted his grip, trying to grasp more than just my coat. I saw a hand thrust towards me and reached for it, while continuing to claw desperately for purchase with my other limbs. Yet it was no effort of mine but the strong hands of the figure above that brought me panting and gasping back to solid ground once more.

I wasn't in the least surprised to recognise Jerry's face.

"Thank you," I managed between hyper-ventilations.

A shout caused me to look back towards the café. Shawna had followed me out after all, if a little belatedly. She was now running across the road towards me. Somewhere between that shout and her arriving, Jerry left.

"What happened? The concern in her voice was a joy.

"Railing gave way. I nearly fell in," I explained, pulling myself a little unsteadily to my feet.

"Shit! Are you okay?"

"Fine now, thanks."

"Who was that with you?"

The question startled me. I was so used to nobody else seeing Jerry that this sign of awareness from Shawna caught me completely off guard. "What?" was my reflexive response.

"When I came out the café there was a figure leaning over you, helping you."

"No." I did my best to look puzzled. "Must have been my coat caught in the wind, or something." Although the garment in question was securely fastened all the way up to the neck.

"I could have sworn I saw someone."

"No," I gestured around expansively, "as you can see, there's nobody else here."

A Question of Timing

I felt like that apostle denying Jesus—which one was it, Peter? And I found myself glancing around, half expecting to spot two further people waiting to be lied to.

Apparently one was enough though, because I've never seen Jerry since.

Two months later, I finally got to fuck Shawna, after she and Aaron split up. I think she turned to me because of that day by the sea; both in the sense that I'd been there at the beginning of their relationship and because of the peculiar bond that formed between us when I so nearly died. This proved to be the only night we spent together. It was nothing special but it was something I suspect we both needed. I'm not sure I even fancied her anymore. My main feeling as we kissed and fumbled and I started to peel off her clothes was one of triumph rather than anticipation. Yet for me, this was the realisation of a long-held ambition and was wholly satisfying as a result, while for her I think it reaffirmed her initial choice of Aaron over me.

I spoke about Jerry that night, as we lay holding each other in the lull between sweaty couplings. Both because she'd seen him that day and because I felt the need to talk about him to *someone*. I'm not sure that she truly understood, but at least she listened. Shawna is the only person I've ever told.

I don't miss Jerry, not really. His absence feels as right as his presence always did. He achieved what he had to, preventing me from going the same way as my brother: too early.

It's all a question of timing, you see. Mine will come, of course, but not yet.

COFFEE BREAK

All he wanted was a cup of coffee.

A simple enough ambition—a goal unlikely to test any man; but on this particular day fate seemed determined to thwart him.

The first indicator was an explosion, which was all Bud Walker needed.

You see, Bud really liked his coffee. Not the tepid, tasteless muck churned out by vending machines, nor the scalded, chicory-bitter excuse for a drink his mom used to make. He liked his coffee just so. Not too bitter, not too mellow; no sugar, thank you very much, but a splash of milk or cream—he wasn't an espresso man, but would accept that rather than have the flavour drowned in a latte. As for cappuccino, well, that was nothing short of a gimmick in Bud's opinion—all froth and no substance.

The coffee bar at the corner of 21st and 7th knew how these things should be done, and this month's fresh blend was pretty close to his idea of coffee heaven.

So when he finally managed to sit down at his usual table near the window, cradling a steaming mug of freshly brewed nectar in front of him, when he was *finally* able to drink in the delicious aroma that curled around his face and tantalised his nostrils, the very last thing he expected to hear was an explosion.

The plate glass beside him shuddered slightly but only just. He glanced out the window at the world beyond and then back at the mug of coffee, considering his options.

The explosion hadn't been *that* close. Granted, it had interrupted one of his favourite moments—savouring the ultimate anticipation

GROWING PAINS

before taking that first sip—but this did not necessarily mean that the entire experience was ruined. He could still recapture the mood, given the chance.

His attention was wrenched outside again by excited yelling almost at his shoulder. A group of people ran quickly past the window in a blur of gangly arms and legs, calling as they went. Kids; a gang of them, perhaps half a dozen strong, running towards the explosion rather than away from it, eager to see what was going on.

Bud turned to look around the coffee bar. He took in the pensive, studious man with the goatee and the polo-neck sweater, intently staring at his laptop, and the two young women at the table opposite, their hands gesturing for emphasis as they exchanged bursts of vapid conversation with the rapidity of machine gun fire, before his eyes came to rest on the queue, which seemed just as long as ever.

They hadn't moved.

They weren't concerned.

Waiting for a decent mug of coffee was still the priority for everyone here.

Reassured, he turned back to his own drink.

Deciding under the circumstances to dispense with the usual formalities, he lifted the mug and took a sip, closing his eyes as the first draught washed into his expectant mouth.

Then came the second explosion.

Louder this time, and closer. The window definitely flexed as opposed to merely thinking about it. Conversation in the coffee bar stuttered to a halt. Not the two young women—Bud suspected that a bomb would need to go off directly under their table in order to claim *their* attention—but everyone else. Even Mr Pensive had been drawn away from his laptop and was looking around worriedly.

Bud swallowed the mouthful of coffee, which went down almost unnoticed, delivering none of the customary pleasure he had been hoping for.

People began to speak again: nervous chatter that seemed to start spontaneously throughout the bar, accompanied by anxious glances towards the street. The man in the black coat at the back of the queue detached himself, evidently deciding that enough was enough. He headed for the door. This was a *big* man, Bud couldn't help but notice. Not that he was exactly svelte himself these days, but this guy moved with a sort of ponderous, exaggerated waddle, which seemed calculated to emphasise his size.

Again Bud's attention was drawn outside by the sound of running feet. More people ran past the window, men and women, glancing over their shoulders with fear in their eyes. At least they were heading in the opposite direction this time, away from the explosions.

Bud took another sip of coffee.

Somebody outside screamed at the same moment as the man from the back of the queue pushed the door open. The scream was immediately followed by the staccato chatter of small arms fire. At this, the dam broke; the queue disintegrated and people started to desert their tables. One woman stood up too quickly, sending her chair clattering over backwards. A child was bowled over in the rush, the first tearful wail emerging even as she was scooped up and consoled by parents eager to depart. Tables rocked and a mug rolled off a surface to smash onto the tiled floor with a strident tinkle of shattered crockery, which was instantly swallowed by the scraping of chairs and the babble of concerned voices, as the exodus became a stampede.

Bud savoured his third swig of coffee, stubbornly refusing to be distracted. He was off duty. This had nothing to do with him.

The only way out of the coffee bar was a single small door, which quickly developed into a bottle neck, stemming the tide of people as they all tried to pile out into the street at once. Bud picked up his mug and shuffled his chair to one side as the jostling mob spread out from the gangway and began to engulf the tables closest to the door, threatening to reach him. They didn't in the end, but you could never be too careful.

The tide of escapees receded as rapidly as it had arisen, with the final stragglers pushing their way through into the outside world. A siren wailed its way rapidly to a *wah-wah* crescendo and back again as a police unit shot past at reckless speed, lording it over a street ominously devoid of traffic. The door swung shut behind the final retreating customer, leaving the bar deserted apart from Bud, the two young women, and the small brigade of white-smocked staff staring out anxiously from behind the counter.

"You see anything?" one of the latter called out.

"No." Bud shook his head. "The street's pretty much deserted now...."

He was interrupted by a figure that came smashing through the big plate glass window at that precise moment, sending shards of glass flying

GROWING PAINS

everywhere, including into Bud's coffee. Bud ducked down beneath the table, not just for protection as some might have thought, but to flip open the twin catches on the large black pilot's case he'd stowed there when he first came in. He realised that the man who had just come through the window didn't represent a threat, principally because the fellow had arrived backwards and head first and hadn't stirred since, but whoever threw him this way still might.

Bud reached calmly into the case and grasped one of the two objects he kept there: his gun, a veritable cannon. He sat up, noting that the new arrival wore a trooper's uniform. The man lay unmoving amongst fragments of glass and scattered tables and chairs.

The gaping window remained apparently empty, but there was a peculiar distortion at the centre of the opening, like a small, localised heat haze. Bud groaned, recognising the effect immediately; a shimmer suit, which almost certainly meant Idalen, and if there was one race in the entire galaxy Bud couldn't stand, it was the Idalen. He looked towards the wall at the opposite side of the room, so that the window was now in the very corner of his vision, lifted his arm across his body, with the gun pointing diagonal to his line of site, and fired. The only way to even begin seeing anything through the shimmer effect was in the corner of your eye.

The alien, visible now that the shimmer suit had been deactivated by its wearer's death, collapsed forward. It's long, tapering frame, disconcertingly manlike in so many ways but oddly stretched and unnaturally slender, lay close to the fallen trooper, who still hadn't moved since his dramatic entrance and probably never would again.

With a sigh, and a single wistful glance at the defiled coffee, Bud reached down to lift the second object out of his case. Cast from a semi-metallic polymer, the helmet was the only piece of kit other than the gun that was portable enough to be carried around. Which meant that he did, even when off duty as he was supposed to be now.

Protection had been very much a secondary consideration in the helmet's design. Sure, it was better than the naked human skull, but we're hardly talking body-armour here. The headpiece's chief reason for being was its built-in software.

Bud slipped the helmet on, secured it, and flipped down the visor. Then he peered out through the smashed window. To his right, two uniformed figures were crouching down by the shell of their disabled cruiser. They were looking this way and that, clearly unsure which direction any threat was likely to come from. Police, not even troopers; they were armed effectively enough but wouldn't be equipped with anything capable of dealing with the eye-foxing effect of a shimmer suit.

Bud scanned the street and thought he spotted a ripple in the air to his left. He adjusted his visor, focussing, until he had the right frequency. Two Idalen leapt into view, strutting along bold as you like, with their stooped forms and exaggerated, heron-like gait, confident that the humans couldn't see them, relying totally on the protection afforded them by their precious shimmer suits.

Neither had even thought to look in his direction. He lifted the gun and fired two quick bursts. Both the aliens went down, though the second one could only have been wounded, because a burst of fire came back at Bud as he stepped out through the shattered window. He instinctively dived to the ground, rolling and firing as he went, though the alien's aim was lousy and its bullets tore at the brickwork high above his head. Neither of the Idalen offered any further threat.

Cursing, Bud got to his feet, brushing dust and glass fragments from his clothes and sucking briefly at a cut finger. The helmet's radio was reporting an Idalen raid on the arms depot at the outskirts of town. The raid had been repulsed, but remnants of the attacking force had escaped and fled into the city.

Great. Why did they have to go and mount a raid during his day off?

Bud started to walk across to the two police officers, who stood uncertainly by their disabled hover-car. The cruiser put him in mind of a beached whale—completely out of its element—sitting there with its field deflated and engines dead. Even the wisps of steam curling up from under its battery hood seemed deliberately designed to taunt him; a cruel parody of the coffee vapours he was being denied.

He had almost reached the stricken vehicle when a further group of Idalen came around the corner to his left.

Bud sprinted the last few steps, yelling out, "Get down," to the two bewildered officers, who, of course, couldn't see the Idalen, so probably thought him crazy. They did as they were told at least, and were scrambling around to the vehicle's far side as Bud joined them.

Bullets were pinging off the cruiser's bodywork as he gave hurried instructions. "Shimmer suits, you know about them?" In response to their terrified nods, he continued, "Good. Shoot where I shoot. You," he indicated the one nearest him, "lay down a pattern of fire around the area my first shot hits, and you, do the same for my second. Got it?" God, they were only kids. What help were they going to be?

More quick woodpecker-nods.

"Okay, come on!"

With that, Bud stood up, peering over the cruiser's roof and firing at the nearest target. Without waiting to see the result, he aimed again and fired towards a group of three approaching figures. The two officers were up beside him, firing blind but as he'd instructed.

Bud counted six of the aliens in all. His first shot had taken out one. His second had missed entirely but the secondary fire from the kid beside him had accounted for another one. That left four. Bud aimed carefully and let loose with a sustained burst.

Three.

Then the kid to his right took a bullet in the shoulder, which flung him back and sent him crashing to the ground.

"Concentrate your fire between those two posters on the wall to the right," Bud yelled to the surviving officer, as he drew a bead on an Idalen that had almost reached them and shot it point blank. The kid got lucky and nailed one of the two remaining ones. But the last alien was right up to them—they moved deceptively quickly on those spindly legs of theirs, flowing across the ground as if on jet-propelled skates.

Bud was twisting around to target this final one, but knew that he was too late, that it had him. He desperately tried to duck down, out of the way, but the Idalen fired at the same instant, and he felt a searing pain across his left temple. Then he hit the ground.

Perhaps he blacked out for a second or two, it was hard to say. He knew that he heard persistent gun fire. Then silence. He looked up when he could, to see the kid still standing, his gun held loosely at his side. Bud scrambled to his feet, aware of fractured vision where his visor had cracked. He made a quick count of Idalen bodies. Six.

"You got it!"

The kid nodded. His face betrayed the surprise he clearly felt at still being alive, the shock at all the violence that had suddenly erupted around him. "I saw where the shot that hit you came from and just emptied my gun at that point."

"Well done," Bud muttered distractedly. He had his helmet off and was tracing a deep crease made by the Idalen bullet as it skidded across his head.

The kid's partner sat up slowly, clutching his bleeding shoulder, only to bend forward and throw up.

Bud remembered his first fire fight and felt a sudden affinity for the lad. He'd thrown up afterwards too.

He gave the wounded man an encouraging smile and the thumbs up, before gingerly putting his helmet back on, aware of the added pressure where it had been bent out of shape by the bullet. At least the audio was still working. He listened, and hoped. His prayers were answered almost immediately, as reports came in that the last of the Idalen attackers had been rounded up and neutralised.

Bud smiled. That hadn't taken too long, all things considered.

More uniforms arrived, tending to the two kids and towing away their wrecked unit. Bud watched as a couple removed the dead trooper from the coffee bar in a zipped-up body bag. The Idalen casualties were too tall for body bags and had to be carted off uncovered.

"We'll need you to come back to the station and make a report," said one of the uniforms, who appeared to be in charge but whose face and name Bud didn't even bother to register.

"Yeah, of course; later," he promised.

Finally they left, allowing Bud to step through the window and back into the coffee bar. Amidst the wreckage, his favourite table was still upright. He brushed shattered glass and debris from its surface and placed his damaged helmet there, then walked resolutely inward. Fractured glass grinding to dust beneath his heel as he strode past scattered chairs and overturned tables, making his way through the whole length of the shop, stopping only once he had reached the counter.

He cleared his throat.

The top of a man's head came slowly into view, its crowning mop of black hair rising to reveal first a broad forehead and then a pair of wide, darting eyes, which peered at him over the edge of the counter. Bud smiled reassuringly, and the figure stood up fully; one of the staff, straightening his white-smock uniform with fastidious care Bud knew most of the guys and girls who regularly served him at this place, but not this one—a short, undistinguished man, older than you normally saw here.

"Is it over?"

GROWING PAINS

"Yup, all done and dusted. I'll have a fresh brew, to drink in; largest you've got, please, and leave room for a dash of milk."

The man stared at him as if he were speaking in an alien tongue. "Are you mad? You saw what just happened. Look at the place. We're not serving coffee. We're closed; *very* closed!"

Bud's smile vanished, his face hardening. "Look, pal, I appreciate this is all a bit upsetting, but let me explain how things are from where I'm standing. You see, I've had a really lousy week. You have no idea just how lousy. And to top it all off, I've had to go and shoot up a bunch of pesky aliens just to get some peace and quiet. Do you know the one thing that's been keeping me going?"

The little man shook his head, the courage that inspired his outburst evidently deserting him. He looked for all the world like a rabbit transfixed by the headlights of an onrushing car.

"The thought of coming in here, of sitting down and taking my time over a cup of your excellent coffee: that's what has seen me through this God-awful week. Now, so far, things may not have gone entirely to plan, but these things happen and that's all behind us now. We can move on, right?"

Bud casually placed his gun down on the counter. Quite by chance, its nozzle was pointing directly at the little man, who gulped visibly and turned as white as a sheet.

"So, how about you fetch me that coffee?" Bud finished, cheerfully.

The man nodded and hurried to comply.

As Bud returned to his seat, one of the two young women emerged hesitantly from the ladies. She saw Bud and seemed to draw strength from his presence, smiling at him and walking out with renewed confidence. He nodded in response. Not bad looking, he acknowledged to himself, now that she'd actually stopped talking.

The other young woman crawled out from under a table, dusted herself down and straightened her dress. She then righted an overturned chair and sat, to be joined almost immediately by her friend.

"Now, where were we?" one said to the other, and they were off again.

Bud tuned out their voices, tuned out the world, then closed his eyes, leant forward, and smelt the coffee.

THE OUTSIDER

DEATH WAS NO SIMPLE PROCESS, confined to a static moment. Life didn't depart at a precise instant, as if responding to the flick of some divine switch, but was wrenched away in jagged stages. There were no Heavenly choirs in attendance and, in place of the gentle slipping-away so often claimed for such occasions, this was a traumatic convulsion, rupturing time's tender fabric and sending shockwaves in every direction; a shattering that flung out fragments of memory with explosive force.

Guided by instinct, The Outsider latched onto one particular shard—driven by an irresistible, all-consuming hunger to follow as the sliver of memory fled inexorably to its source.

A lifetime ago, Hunger flowed into the room.

It crept in around the margins of the door, poured in through the ventilation system and seeped in through the porous bricks of the walls. Not a mote of dust was disturbed and no draft arose to betray its arrival, yet Hunger continued to gather until its presence filled the place.

Here it paused, basking in the surrounding echoes—the resonance of what had been, preserved by the dim memory of the room. This was an abandoned building scheduled for demolition, which until recently had been part of a hospital, a delivery room for the maternity unit. A place of beginning, of many beginnings.

Over the course of decades life after life had made the traumatic transition from womb to world in this room. Along with life emotions had been born; raw and powerful feelings that repeatedly poured forth to saturate the surrounds, permeating the very fabric of walls, floor and ceiling. Here mothers had stoically struggled through the exhausting

GROWING PAINS

peaks and troughs of agony and joy, of body-ripping strain and blessed relief, whilst fathers had contributed their own kaleidoscope of anxiety, concern, pride and pleasure.

The room was now just a desiccated shell, a fragile vessel of distant memory, but that was enough.

To Hunger's perception time was not entirely linear—past and future reverberated into the now. Anchored in the present but not strictly bound by it, Hunger's essence sampled the echoes of what had already happened and what was yet to come.

Though only the past mattered here.

It sifted through the complex soup of emotions that still lingered in the room, searching for one specific cluster of feelings: those that had drawn the shard of death-memory here. It isolated them from the numerous intertwined knots of emotional extreme and drew them forth, assimilating them into its very being.

With them came identity, or at least the beginnings of one. It was a 'he' and he was K.

K flowed swiftly away, still hungry.

Another emotional nexus: K arrived at an austere, compartment-riddled building, drawn to a single room, a classroom. Though still in use the place was empty at this time of night. Here were the earliest memories of school—the wrenching fear as his mother walked away that first day, the panic of abandonment. A child cast adrift in a strange new world, bereft of accustomed reference points and comforts, at a loss as to what was expected of him and uncertain of how he was supposed to cope with this terrifying new environment.

All of this was absorbed. K grew a little more complete. He was now Ken and Ken moved on.

The hunger was still there and would stay with him, relentlessly goading until assimilation was complete, but he was now more than just hunger, more than simply one single overriding drive. Now he was beginning to reason. With reason came a riddle: why was he alone here? On such a ripe and vulnerable world, why could he sense no others of his kind?

Another hospital in another town. Here his sister had been born: his parents' greatest betrayal.

He felt again the bitter resentment at this usurper, the intense jealousy that had never quite left him. It was impossible to be certain how much of that jealousy had been felt here at the birth and how much had developed during the months and years that followed—the emotional paths were too confused, too tangled—but they all led from this instant. His relationship with his mother had changed at this point. They would never be as close again.

There followed a series of places, of emotional surges, with pain far outweighing joy, yet all were welcomed into his consciousness, all added to his growing sense of self.

Here he had first kissed a girl—a clumsy meeting of tongues, lips and teeth, a parting sloppy with saliva. It was a disappointing prelude to his sexual life.

There he had first ventured a hand beneath a girl's skirt, fingers groping blindly into the unknown. She was more experienced than he and had little patience with his inept fumblings. She had squealed as his clumsy explorations hurt her and slapped his hand away, wriggling from his embrace. He remembered her standing in front of him, lashing his ego with some caustic remark, the precise words now lost in time and not worth the effort of recalling, before straightening her skirt and stalking away, displaying her contempt with every indignant stride.

The following day at school had been a living hell, with the girl and her friends whispering and sniggering as he passed. He imagined the whole school knew of the previous night's disaster. By the end of the day a good proportion of it did, as the girls grew bolder and their taunts more open. It led to another girl's tears: the one he was supposed to be going out with. He could no longer even recall her face, except that she left the impression of being homely and innocent, in marked contrast to his chief tormentor—the sexy and sassy girl he had been kissing the previous evening.

The hurt he had caused his 'girlfriend' was irrelevant at the time. All he could see was his own humiliation, not someone else's pain.

In any case, she could not have been too badly hurt; certainly not enough to prevent her from becoming the first girl he actually fucked, less than two weeks later.

He remembered her kisses had tasted of spearmint and she had left a love-bite on his shoulder.

For both of them this had been the first time; an awkward, ill-judged encounter which neither took much pleasure in. An experiment; a

GROWING PAINS

release of tension for him and perhaps little more than that for her. It was never repeated, nor did either of them refer to it again. The next day they hardly spoke and within a month they were barely friends.

Now Kenneth was drawn to a house—a respectable, detached family home in a much sought-after suburban area, complete with ornate porch and prominent bay window. He was in the master bedroom, gazing at the bed, perhaps even the very same bed in which he had experienced sex with a woman for the second and last time. She was a neighbour, one of his parents' friends; an attractive and glamorous married mother of two—the stuff of a teenage boy's wet dreams. Here he discovered passion in an encounter that could not have been more different from his first time. Here he learnt the contrast between a woman and a girl. In terms of her knowledge and experience, her scent, her kisses, her touch, the very curves of her body, there was no comparison between this and that earlier awkward joining. It was like making love to a completely different sex, a different species. He had come almost immediately—an embarrassment that she brushed aside, coaxing and caressing him back to firmness. The second and third times he lasted much longer.

He was never really certain why she seduced him. Perhaps on a whim, perhaps just to prove that she could, or perhaps it was so that she could feel superior to his mother in some perverse way, as they sipped coffee and nattered about the latest neighbourhood scandal. As far as Kenneth was aware his mother never learned of their indiscretion. Perhaps it was just for the kick, the illicit thrill.

He turned fifteen a few weeks later.

His first time had left him with the conviction that sex was overrated, or perhaps was simply not for him, but this had been a revelation, a moment of pure delight to be savoured and treasured.

For a while he imagined he was in love with her and dreamt of the two of them running away and making a life together. In the face of her subsequent indifference the dream withered and died, as had so much else in his life.

Kenneth J. left the house, the street, the town, and found himself drawn to a glow on the horizon, which resolved itself into a myriad of artificial lights burning fiercely in the night. A larger town, a city even. Here was a street infested with twin lines of multi-coloured cars, barely moving, sitting bumper-to-bumper like coloured beads on a child's necklace, engines growling impatiently. Leading off the street was a darkened alleyway in which stood a door with a gaggle of youths queuing outside. A club; a heaving mass of sweat and energy, with bouncers standing at discreet and not-so discrete vantage points, making sure the customers behaved themselves.

Here he had first kissed a man, tasting nicotine and lager. Here he had first acknowledged that he was never destined to find fulfilment with a woman. Yet he had left the club alone, shaken and confused.

Onward.

A hotel room. His face half-buried in the pillow, awareness of a presence above and behind him... a man, pressing against him, then into him.... the thrill, the pain, the excitement, the fear and the joy as he was penetrated for the first time, with every thrust that followed a bitter sweet hybrid of pleasure and pain.

A stranger. It had to be with a stranger this first time. That way, if he hated the experience, if this proved to be yet another instance on the conveyor-belt of life's disappointments, no one need ever know. It would just be a failed experiment that left the rest of his existence untouched.

He never saw the man again.

The places, the memories and emotions, came thick and fast now, as Kenneth John picked up the pace.

There was the party thrown in honour of his sister, when she succeeded in reaching Cambridge. His parents' unabashed pride at their 'clever one'; family and friends gathered to celebrate all that she had achieved. Choking rage at the unfairness of it all, jealousy a solid core of ice within him, scarring heart and soul. He had failed to fully join in the spirit of the occasion and had thrown a moody, a tantrum of petulance and spite, knowing even at the time that he appeared churlish as a result.

Next came the violent row with his father when he was 'outed' as gay. The violence had been verbal and in posture only, but had threatened to spill over into the physical. He relived the pitiful sight of his mother sitting on the settee, sobbing, hands pressed to her cheeks as she implored them both to stop, to calm down. He remembered the savage joy at hurting and shocking them so deeply; payback for all their betrayal, all the times they had failed him. Yet at the same time something had broken and withered inside him.

GROWING PAINS

Eventually his father came around. They reached an unspoken understanding—a rigid and distant acceptance that excluded paternal love ever after. His mother was more understanding. She tried to love him despite it all. The effort was painful for both of them.

His sister just seemed to view him with disdain, but there was nothing new in that.

Then it was his mother's funeral. Many of the same faces that had populated his sister's party, but older and all kitted out in monochrome. The loss of his mother hit him far less than anticipated. In a sense he had been losing her for years. There was grief, but more for the memories of childhood and for the closeness that had slipped away. There was also anger, because she was deserting both life and him, but again it was less than he would have expected, perhaps because this was just the final act of a betrayal that had started with his sister's conception.

Then on to a darkened bedroom. Again he reached across time, drawing forth the memories of a party held in this house, of his sitting in this very room. Here he had first dabbled with hard drugs. His then boyfriend was a user who eventually persuaded him to experiment, but for him the syringe held only horror, a loss of control that he hated, an experience that he chose not to dwell on. Ever the outsider, it was a path he would not venture down again. He split with the boyfriend soon after.

Next it was another bar, where he had spent a long evening sipping designer beers at inflated prices. This was the type of place he always avoided—too trendy, too shallow, too expensive—but it had been perversity's day, bittersweet if ever a day could be. He had just lost his job, proving that it *was* a job as opposed to the career he had previously imagined it to be. 'Rationalisation', 'downsizing', 'current economic climate'—there was nothing original about the reasons or the excuses. At one level he was shocked; he had believed himself to be good at what he did, indispensable even. At another level it was no surprise whatsoever. This was life, after all.

Yet in the midst of his self-pity, hope had appeared. This was where and when he first met Adam. Breath-catchingly handsome Adam, whose grey-blue eyes were a Velcro trap—once their gaze held you it was near-impossible to tear yourself free. Adam: so animated, so vital, that all other company seemed dull and mundane by comparison. Adam, who talked openly of long-term relationships with partners of both sexes in the past and whose magnetism invariably drew attention from people of both genders wherever he went

In the months that followed, Kenneth Johnson was to watch him flirt outrageously with both men and women, but in an amusing and harmless way. He never felt threatened by any of that. He trusted Adam; not something he could have said about many people during the course of his life. So this was a day that had combined both disappointment and great joy.

Kenneth R. Johnson was almost complete. Only one last nexus remained—the most telling of all.

His home; an elegant second floor apartment in an up-and-coming part of town, which he had shared for the last six months with Adam, the first man he trusted enough to live with. The first man he thought he might love.

All that had changed tonight, of course.

There was no reason for him to enter the flat quietly, but then there was no reason for him to make a noise, either. He had no idea what drew him straight to the bedroom; perhaps some slight noise. As he approached the closed door the sound became unmistakeable. It was the sound of a couple making love. He paused outside the room, staring at the door handle, almost not going in, almost turning round and walking away, wanting to come back later and pretend he had heard nothing.

But instead his hand reached out, without his consciously willing it. The door opened and he stepped inside.

They had their backs to him. The tableau reminded him of his first time with a man in that long-ago hotel room. A figure lying on its stomach, face pressed against the pillow and a man behind, on his knees, pelvis thrusting rhythmically.

Except that the man thrusting was Adam and the person lying on the bed was a woman.

Tumble of long blonde hair. Even before she turned her head, he knew who it was.

His sister saw him first, Adam not realising until seconds later, presumably alerted by some change, some tensing of the body he was fucking.

He met Adams eyes for an unbearable instant and then turned and walked from the room, not saying a word.

His sister followed him out, calling his name. He sat on the chair—

GROWING PAINS

his usual, familiar chair. She stood before him, clutching a blanket across one breast—his blanket—an inadequate and irrelevant shield for her modesty.

Kenneth Rich Johnson heard sounds. Words themselves were discernable here, spoken so recently that their echo remained strong.

"God I'm so sorry... never meant it to happen. I came to see you, but you weren't here. Got chatting to Adam, we opened some wine..." and "You know what he's like, so funny. We were both flirting a bit and then we were kissing." Followed by "I don't know what came over me. Please say you forgive me. I didn't mean to hurt you. You know I'd never hurt you." Finally, "I'd... I'd better go," and "Please don't tell Maurice," her husband. She moved uncertainly back to the bedroom.

Throughout it all he sat unmoving, staring straight ahead, looking through her rather than at her, refusing to acknowledge her existence.

He heard them whispering in the bedroom, neither knowing nor caring what was said. She emerged first, now fully dressed. She hovered over him. "For God's sake say something. Scream at me, swear at me, whatever you fucking want. I deserve it, I know I do, but don't just sit there ignoring me." He did nothing, felt nothing... just an all-encompassing numbness. For a moment it seemed that she might cry or perhaps even hit him, but instead she settled for shrieking an exasperated "Oh, screw you!" and stalked to the front door. There she paused, apparently regretting her loss of control. "I'm sorry," the calm, reasonable voice he knew so well. "Look, I really am sorry. I'll call you," and she was gone.

Only then did Adam put in an appearance.

Only then did he react. An explosion of pain and anger, venting a lifetime's worth of suppressed frustration and rage born of self-failure and perceived betrayal, all focused on this one moment, this one person whom he had valued enough to trust.

He threw Adam out, of course, barely allowing enough time for bags to be packed.

"Where do you expect me to go?"

Not his problem.

He half expected his own tears, but there were none. He had never been one to cry much, even when very young.

He felt emptied, finished. Nothing in the world had any meaning; nothing was worth this amount of pain.

He had no idea how many pills would be needed and was determined not to take too few, so he swallowed the entire contents of the bottle. This was not a cry for help. He had no desire to be noticed or loved. He wanted to end it, to close the door once and for all on the relentless burden of living, of coping with the drudgery, the bleakness and the never-ending hurt which seemed to be all that life had to offer.

So he took the pills and waited.

Was one bottle enough? It was all he had. Waiting had never been his strong point. What if he only went into a deep sleep? What if he was discovered and revived? He went to the bathroom and ran the bath, feeling suddenly light-headed. Sleep was approaching, but how final would it be? Panicking a little, he snatched up the new chef's knife from the kitchen, its blade keen enough to split hairs, and hurried back to the bathroom, where he started to pull off his clothes. The room began to waver—a disconcerting shift that took everything out of focus and back again. The world had acquired a surreal edge.

He had to sit down in order to pull his socks off, dropping onto the toilet seat to do so. His field of vision started to contract, as if blinkers were slowly closing in. Everything blurred and he knew he would not be able to stand again.

It was his final memory, as he collapsed off the toilet to lie sprawled on the bathroom floor.

Kenneth Richard Johnson stood in the bathroom, looking down upon his lifeless body. Assimilation was complete. Too complete.

All the anguish and stress of a tormented soul had become part of his very being. He had encompassed and accepted as his own every nuance, every self-inflicted wound of a bitter life. Never on a hundred different worlds had he encountered such a depth of despair. How could sentient beings live like this?

His kind spent uncounted ages adrift in darkness—nebulous clouds of energy strung out across the vastness of space, little denser than vacuum itself, pulled by the barely tangible tug of distant sentience. On reaching an inhabited world they were drawn to the recently dead, focusing on a death not yet discovered, a life that could be assimilated, a being that could be replaced. They would then continue with the interrupted life, merging seamlessly with the native population.

GROWING PAINS

They did not kill, they were not predators but opportunists—parasites who feasted on emotions, the flavour of feelings which were unique to each inhabited world and helped to shape the nature of sentience. Once they were sated, once they had sampled all that a given people had to offer, they would move on, returning to space, dispersing their tenuous substance as widely as possible, searching for the faintest telltale hint of the next host planet.

He had done this a hundred times or more, yet nothing in his experience had prepared him for such burdens, for the overwhelming depression that now assaulted his soul. Nothing previously encountered had prepared him for this; for becoming Kenneth Richard Johnson . . . for becoming human.

Somewhere along the way humanity's social evolution had become irretrievably twisted. Inexplicably they had developed a society that, rather than enhancing an individual's life, placed them under intolerable psychological pressure and strain. He had no idea how humanity coped with the despair that must blight each and every one of them, but he knew for certain that his own species could not; that he could not.

Assimilation took little time, for all its darting from place to place and absorption of memory and emotion, but neither was it instantaneous. He tested the water in the bath; still warm, but not hot. He needed hot. So he pulled the plug and watched as the water drained away, listening to it flow through the pipes until half the volume had vanished. Only then did he replace the plug and start to refill with fresh, hot water. The chef's knife still rested on the edge of the bath, where the previous Kenneth Richard Johnson . . . where he had left it, earlier that evening.

He stepped into the bath, unprepared for the scalding kiss of the water. Still he sat, easing himself down gently. For long moments he remained unmoving, familiarising himself with the heavy darkness that now sat at the core of his being; a coil of rage and anger and frustration and despair beyond his imagining.

There was no choice. He stretched his arms out before him, under the water. Then he reached to take the knife in his right hand, drawing its blade swiftly across his submerged left wrist. There was surprisingly little pain. Even as a red cloud started to blossom around his hand he transferred the knife and repeated the action on his other wrist. Twin red plumes now spread before him.

He sat back, closed his eyes and concentrated on feeling nothing.

This was a world of the insane, where a balanced intelligence could never hope to survive. He no longer wondered why there were no others of his kind here—it was self explanatory.

Soon, there were none at all.

Hobbies

Every day Josh thanked his lucky stars that he had been born into this particular age at this particular time. Never before had information and technology been so easy to get hold of, which provided him with everything he needed to pursue his hobby.

He sat now, basking in sunshine, feeling its warmth on his neck as he leant forward, taking each precision-crafted component from his valise and assembling the gun with unhurried efficiency. The penultimate piece to be clipped into place was the scope—a true marvel, with digital zoom and every kind of image enhancement that man could devise. That left just the final element—the ammo clip.

He inspected the completed weapon with critical eye, proud to be its owner. Satisfied, he glanced up at a near-cloudless sky, savouring the fact that he was outdoors while pitying all those people who scurried around the city's streets, heads down and shoulders bowed with the weight of quarterly targets, impending budget cutbacks, the need to qualify for performance-related bonuses, or the sheer monotony of the daily grind: house to car to train to office and back. How many of them ever took time out to simply pause and glance up at the sky? How many of them were even likely to notice what a beautiful day it was?

Of course, that was where *he* came in. Josh saw himself as a renegade factor within the system, there to disrupt the mundane, to break the conveyor belt of daily routine and to make the masses think about the wider picture, the world outside their own little bubble.

He lay down on his stomach, wriggling to get comfortable. It was important to be comfortable, to be relaxed. The gun was in position, both he and it peering over the lip of the building's roof. From here Josh

GROWING PAINS

had an unrestricted view of a large paved square bracketed by corporate offices, perhaps half a mile away.

Figures criss-crossed the space in apparent Brownian motion, each intent on their own inscrutable errand and oblivious to all else.

Josh peered through the scope and the scene leapt towards him. With deft adjustment things came closer still and he was able to make out individual faces, all bearing frowns of concentration or steely-eyed stares of determined purpose. Not a smile to be seen anywhere. He adjusted the scope again until his field of vision covered the whole of the square.

There was no huge rush. He watched intently, waiting for two suitable subjects to walk into view and at last they did, one from either side. He gave them time to move closer to each other, narrowing the field of focus as they merged. Judging them to be close enough, he zoomed in, focusing on the figure to the right: a man in blue business suit, with slick black hair and small frameless spectacles.

One long breath to steady himself, and then he gently caressed the trigger, drawing it towards him until his shoulder felt the playful push of dampened recoil. The silencer reduced the sound to something closer to a kiss than a gunshot; Josh's very own kiss of death.

Instantly he adjusted, swivelling the gun a fraction to his left, to find the redhead frozen in horror. Even as he set himself she moved, backing away. Realising she might bolt, or freeze, or even go forward to help the fallen man, that her movements were no longer wholly predictable, he decided to forego his preferred head-shot, adjusting for a wider focus. Her torso came into view, her pale blue summer top and bare arms, a hand pressed to her mouth as if to suppress a scream. He fired and then waited to watch her go down.

She was still moving, trying to crawl away, so Josh refocused and this time took the head shot.

He scooped up the three spent cases and quickly pulled himself and the gun away from the edge, on his stomach the whole way. Only when he reached the still-open case did he sit up and dismantle the gun, a well-practised process that took mere seconds. Then he was on his feet, brushing himself down as he headed for the door and the stairs beyond.

The sounds, the screaming, reached him as if from a great distance, seeming surreal and detached as a result.

HOBBIES

At the bottom of the short flight of steps, Josh hesitated, peering out to make sure the corridor was clear before stepping out of the service door. Then it was a brief walk to the elevator, a moment of growing frustration as he waited for it to arrive, followed by a study of unconcerned nonchalance as a man joined him three floors later.

"Lovely day," the newcomer observed.

Josh relaxed a little and smiled, glad that at least one other person had noticed. "Yes, yes it is," he agreed.

The first thing he saw as he stepped out of the building was a police unit; though it wasn't there for him but was rather straining to make progress along the congested street amid heavy traffic. Drivers were trying to inch their vehicles this way and that to accommodate its passage, but there was nowhere for them to go. The car's strident siren masked any other sounds. Josh glanced towards it, but no more than anyone else did. He ducked down into the subway entrance and the siren became muted and was soon inaudible.

The police would be trying to second guess him, he knew that—scratching their sweaty heads as they sought to work out the system he was using to select his targets. Good luck to them. He had a system all right, in fact he had several. Today it was people wearing blue. Last week it was people on the right-hand side of a group from his viewpoint, and two weeks before that it had been anyone with blond hair.

Josh had done his homework, planning for months before he even considered indulging his hobby. Again, the availability of technology and information proved invaluable. He studied the blueprints of more than a hundred buildings, drawing up a list of all those that were tall enough and had roofs which promised to be readily accessible. He then visited each and every one, to assess all the factors and detail that the blueprints couldn't provide, such as the level of security, how easy it was to reach and leave the roof without drawing attention, how close the nearest subway entrance. And most importantly of all, did the roof provide a good view over a suitable killing field?

The subway car was pretty full but not packed and after a single stop he found a seat. The girl sitting opposite was fiddling with some toy or other, which she managed to drop. It was one of those small gizmos that can transform itself into half a dozen different animals at the touch of a control stud. Currently, it was in the default state of a ball. So when it hit the floor the thing bounced and then rolled, crossing the short distance across the carriage and coming to rest by Josh's foot. He bent down and picked the toy up, handing it across to the uncertain looking girl, offering her a warm smile as he did so. The mother smiled back and thanked him before lecturing her daughter on being more careful with her toys.

They were both wearing blue.

The mother flashed a smile at him again as she shepherded the little girl off the train a few stops later, in what might have been a come-on. She was pretty enough and Josh wondered briefly whether he had just missed an opportunity. Not that it mattered; he was intent on far bigger kicks than sweaty sex, whether seasoned with infidelity or not.

He came out of the subway on the far side of town, entering a building all but interchangeable with the first. This time around the elevator ride was more typical, with the few people who stepped in and out staring fixedly at the floor or the doors, intent on keeping themselves to themselves.

He was the last one off. The door leading to the service stairs stood directly next to the elevator shaft, enabling him to step through without drawing anyone's attention. Clouds had rolled in to spasmodically obscure the sun and it was generally cooler, with the wind gusting at him as he pieced the gun together.

He had chosen this one deliberately, because it was a long way from the first building and also because it offered an easy shot. The view was straight along the length of a wide and busy street. He lay down, fidgeted, and sighted through the scope, focussing on the steady stream of people crossing his field of vision where a major road bisected this one. It was the first time he had hit two locations in the same day. Another fresh element for those hunting him to take into account and puzzle over.

Josh knew that this was going to have to be as swift and efficient as he could make it—no room for any slip ups. The added pressure weighed upon him and he found himself unable to enjoy the operation as much as usual. Perhaps this would turn out to be the one and *only* time he tried two different spots consecutively.

He forced himself to calm down, to breathe deeply, to not take a shot at the first person to walk across his view wearing something vaguely blue, but to wait for the right subject—one who presented a clear target, not obscured by other pedestrians. One who felt right.

Eventually she strolled into view; middle-aged, dyed blonde hair and wearing a powder blue jacket. Josh took an instant dislike to the woman and knew that killing her would be a pleasure.

In the end, despite his initial misgivings, the kick was still there: the near-sexual rush as he gently pulled the trigger and felt the gun ejaculate its single potent fruit unerringly towards the target, dealing death far more reliably than any given sperm could bestow life.

No, *more* than sexual, he corrected himself.

His departure from roof and building went without incident. Josh was buzzing like never before, despite or even because of the earlier sense of pressure. Perhaps he *would* try two sites again at some point, or maybe even three. He glanced around at the other people in the crowded subway car and knew that any one of them could be his subject next time. The knowledge gave him a private sense of superiority. A pretty brunette locked eyes with him for a second and then looked away with what Josh interpreted as a dismissive sneer. He smiled, content in the knowledge that one day soon he might hold her life in his hand, at the tip of his trigger finger.

A kid was staring at him. Pale caramel brown skin, tight curled black hair and a face that was dominated by the oddest pink visor. Not shades, not ski-goggles, but something else. The kid's eyes locked with his through the pinkness and it was Josh who looked away first, pretending to read one of the blandishments that interspersed the subway maps above the carriage window.

He passed the time in wondering whether the kid was wearing anything blue beneath that black coat.

It was only a short distance from the station to his door and he walked it in a state of euphoric excitement, all but oblivious to his surroundings.

Only at the very last second did he register the presence of a looming figure behind him, an instant before he felt the press of sharp steel at his throat and a hand gripping his arm.

"Do as I say and nobody gets hurt," said the voice at his ear: a rasping, urgent voice. Joshua had little doubt who the 'nobody' referred to was.

He found himself bustled into an alleyway and slammed face-first into a wall, the knife now pressed against the edge of neck and throat.

"Don't look round" his attacker warned.

GROWING PAINS

Joshua kept a tight grip on his case and held it protectively sandwiched between the wall and his calf. He could accept losing anything, but not his gun.

"Put the case down," the voice said, as if reading his thoughts.

Josh froze, unwilling to obey and not knowing how to react.

The pressure of blade on neck abruptly increased. "Do it!"

"Please, no, not my case."

Again the pressure increased and Josh felt the knife cut into his flesh. In sudden fear and almost against his own volition, he let go, feeling the valise slip from beneath his leg and tumble to the ground. A single bead of blood welled up from the shallow cut and trickled down his neck, its passage barely noted in his horror at relinquishing the case.

"Stupid bastard."

The knife was suddenly gone from his throat as the mugger bent down. Josh looked around to see a mop of dark, tight-curled hair and a well-built youth who was stooping to retrieve the case. He could have acted then, could have turned and kicked out while the other was bent over and off-balance... But he froze. This was no clinical dispatching with a sniper's rifle. This was violence.

The instant of opportunity passed as the kid looked up. Pink shades, remembered from the subway train. In them, and in the eyes behind them, them Josh saw his own death.

"I told you not to look round," the kid snarled, leaping up.

Josh caught a flash of steel in the corner of his eye and tried to raise a hand to protect his face, but too late. The blade slashed across his throat.

Jay looked down at the body and felt no remorse. The idiot had seen his face; of course he had to die.

He didn't bother going through the pockets, wasn't interested in the wallet or the cell phone and made no attempt to take the corpse's watch. Jay couldn't have cared less about any of those—he could get their like anywhere. He simply snatched up the case from where it had fallen, staring at it greedily.

He touched the side of his visor, adjusting the focus, and for the first time looked at the case itself. There was nothing extraordinary about it; just a smart, unremarkable valise. He touched the visor again, and smiled.

As soon as he had heard about these visors Jay knew he had to have one, scrimping and scraping for months until he had enough and then immediately buying one on the cheap from the internet, before he could blow the money on anything else.

He knew nothing about how the thing worked or who manufactured it, beyond the advertising blurb's claim that its origins were somehow connected with NASA—a spin-off from technology developed during the space program. Who cared? All that Jay was interested in was that the device worked as promised, which it undeniably did.

With the visor on, he could peer inside just about anything and so was able to see whatever anyone was carrying. It was a mugger's dream.

Jay adored this age of accessible technology. After all, without it, he would never have been able to pursue his hobby, his obsession. How else could someone like him ever afford to collect guns?

This latest one looked to be a real beauty.

Shop Talk

Gemma had obviously been running; she was gasping for breath and her eyes in the doorscreen gleamed with excitement. Calli waited for a few seconds, watching with amusement as her friend shifted impatiently from foot to foot, before instructing the house to admit her.

"There's a new shop in town," Gemma said breathlessly as she came in, not even bothering to say 'hello'.

A new shop? Perhaps the day was not going to prove such a non-event after all.

"Really? What's it stock?"

"Clothes."

"Oh." Another one. For a moment there she had been fooled by Gemma's excitement into hoping for the unusual.

"No, trust me, you want to see this. The clothes are zero degrees."

"Oh sure." Calli gave a disdainful toss of her head. "As if clothes could ever be *that* cool?"

"These are. Really!" Gemma's voice betrayed her. She was clearly desperate to share her new discovery and at the same time afraid of being dismissed as a dweeb for getting so worked up over mere clothes.

Calli said nothing, just raised her eyebrows to produce her best 'I'm only tolerating you at this precise moment' look.

"Oh please, Cal." Gemma was openly pleading now. "You must come and see them. They're strange, they're wonderful . . . they're just so different."

It seemed that in the space of a moment the conversation had evolved into a personal crusade for Gemma, so determined was she to

GROWING PAINS

vindicate her enthusiasm. Calli felt a sudden mischievous urge to refuse, but dismissed the thought even as it occurred to her.

Instead she shrugged and smiled. "Okay, I'll come—if only to shut you up." After all, there was nothing better to do.

The two girls strolled out of the house, leaving it to seal itself and power down, through the wooden gate in the white picket fence and into the lane, heading towards town. Gemma, who was a head shorter than Calli, slightly stout to her slender, and dark blonde to her brunette, was gushing—initially with gratitude and then from sheer excitement.

"There's this old man that runs the place. He's a bit creepy, but don't worry, just ignore him..."

Calli tuned out the other's voice and concentrated on simply enjoying the walk. It was a lovely day, exactly as WET (the Weather Engineering Trust) had promised. Things had gone pretty smoothly since they took over running the climate a couple of years ago. The previous lot, ECC (the Environment Control Consortium) had been a shambles—you never knew whether to pack a sunhat or an umbrella, whatever they scheduled.

Her dad had moaned constantly about ECC. "Don't know how they got the job, it's a disgrace... How are the old land farmers supposed to cope when they've no idea what's coming? Just be grateful we're firmly in hydroponics."

Hydroponics: her future. How she hated that word.

"Lovely afternoon, isn't it girls?" She glanced up to see the craggy smile of Davy Arthur.

They were passing the old school house and Davy was lounging in the shade of its porch, pushing himself gently back and forth on a flimsy-looking rocker. Everyone knew Davy Arthur—he had been the town gardener for as long as Calli could remember. Now that she took the trouble, she could hear the persistent hum of the half dozen mini-cutters he was currently supervising. The bird-sized 'bots were busy trimming the long privet hedge into neat uniformity, buzzing around its crown like giant metallic beetles, their silver carapaces glinting in the sun.

A tall figure emerged from the whitewashed building behind the old gardener. Calli's heart sank; it was Matt, Davy's son. Why did they have to bump into him of all people?

"Hello, Calli."

"Matt," she acknowledged curtly.

"Just teaching Matt here the trade," Davy explained with obvious pride.

"Hello, Matt."

"Hi, Gemma."

Despite the greeting being so clearly an afterthought, Gemma went all moon-faced and stood there with such a ridiculous grin that Calli feared she was about to start drooling.

"Must dash," she said, taking hold of her friend firmly by the elbow and propelling her in the direction of town. "There's this great new shop I simply *have* to see."

"I heard about that shop," Davy Arthur called after them. "You be careful; it's from out-of-town, you know."

The comment was so unexpected that Calli almost stopped and asked what he meant, but then she remembered Matt and strode on with greater purpose.

"What an odd thing to say," she murmured.

"Did you see the way Matt looked at me?" Gemma asked.

Calli managed not to utter any of the several tempting responses that leapt to mind and, for once, stayed quiet. At least her friend's new preoccupation had stopped her wittering on about the wretched shop and its clothes.

Progress became disjointed once they reached the town proper, as they paused to exchange greetings first with the Gallagher twins, then with Mrs. Clement and again with Mr. Turnbull, who nearly bowled them over as he strode with unaccustomed haste out of a shop, clutching his latest purchase like some newly discovered treasure.

"Look," he urged, eagerly thrusting his prize forward for them to admire.

It was all Calli could manage not to physically recoil from the leather-bound lump and its musty smell.

They were outside the bookshop, she realised, with its austere brickwork façade and its leaded-glass windows in mock-wood frames, complete with flaking paint. The venerable old shop had been a feature of the town for over a month now. Not that either girl had deigned to set foot inside—they would never be seen dead in a place like that.

GROWING PAINS

"Real paper, mind, none of your digital rubbish," Turnbull was saying. "Used to be in the library at the Vatican, this book did."

Suddenly Calli found the prospect of looking at clothes—*any* clothes—highly exciting.

They excused themselves, an impatient Gemma tugging at Calli's hand, and ran off down the street, giggling.

"Books? Can you believe it?" Gemma exclaimed when they were safely out of earshot.

"I know. How many people down the centuries do you suppose have read that thing? Just the thought of all those grubby hands pawing over the words and turning the pages gives me the creeps... unhygienic or what?"

"Gross!"

The girls stopped, suddenly aware of a vibration rapidly building through the air as well as the ground—a deep humming that crept towards a whine, climbing perceptibly in both pitch and volume as they listened.

The singing crystal shop, Calli realised. It was about to leave. She turned to find that its windows were already opaque, and continued to watch as the shop began to shimmer, waiting for the vibration to reach a crescendo—which it did almost at once, cutting off abruptly with a sharp 'pop' as air rushed into the sudden void. The shop had vanished, leaving an empty lot in its place, ready for the next retailer.

"I wonder where it's going," she said wistfully.

"The Middle East," replied Mrs. Lundy, who must have joined them whilst she was preoccupied, "and then on to China. They'll be back in the spring though, stocked with the finest crystals from around the world, Sunita promised."

The two girls exchanged glances. They had visited the singing crystal shop together when it first arrived and formed a shared opinion of its wares: same old tat given an exotic spin.

Calli even harboured doubts about the shopkeeper, suspecting that her skin colour was artificially augmented to enhance the exotic image. Her real name was probably Sharon.

"Come on," Gemma said as soon as Mrs. Lundy had continued on her way, "it's just around the corner."

And there it was—a small, neat shop-front, nestling between the Instant Eatery and Ernie's Entertainment Emporium, looking quite at home. Calli tried to remember what had been there immediately before, but couldn't.

The large plate-glass window displayed a single item: a beautiful flowing white dress of unusual cut and semi-translucent material, worn by a mannequin which walked casually on the spot, simulating a stroll along a sandy beach, the dress rippling in some imperceptible breeze. Simple and elegant. Class.

Gemma pushed the door open and beckoned her to follow. To her own considerable surprise, Calli was hooked even before she stepped inside.

She sensed at once that this was a friendly shop, that it would welcome your browsing through its stock all day if you chose to. And what stock. A mesmerising array of clothing confronted her, causing her eye to flit like a confused butterfly from one point to another, uncertain where to settle.

"Welcome, young ladies, welcome." A portly middle-aged man approached, his face lit by a dazzling smile. There was something odd about that face and it took Calli a moment to work out what it was: glasses, he was wearing old-fashioned glasses. Talk about taking an image to extreme. Yet, somehow, they worked, and managed to perch atop the bridge of his nose as if they belonged there.

"You arrive at a most propitious moment," the man continued. Calli realised that he had introduced himself but she had failed to catch the name—Donovan or some such. "The shop is about to give birth."

The two girls stared at each other in horror. "As in a *baby* shop . . . ?"

"Good gracious, no." The shopkeeper sounded as shocked as they felt. "That really would be something to see!" He chuckled. "To a new line of clothes."

"Oh, right."

"Cool."

Relief all round.

"They should be ready in a few minutes but in the meantime please look around." He gestured expansively, the sweep of his arm taking in a whole wall of outfits.

"Oh wow, look at this, Cal," said Gemma, who was already on the case.

She held out an iridescent costume, which pulsed with shades of purple and blue, ripples of colour which coursed soothingly across the

GROWING PAINS

material as it moved. Calli went for a closer look but was distracted by another item—a bright orange sarong in a lacy material that proved deceptively substantial when she ran her hand along it.

"You have a good eye," said Donovan beside her.

She turned to see the man's round face once more graced with a warm and infectious smile that lent it genuine charm. She found herself smiling back and decided that she liked this portly shopkeeper. Could this really be the same person Gemma had described as creepy?

"What is it?" she asked, holding up the sarong. "I've never seen anything like it."

"No, you wouldn't have. This is Selith pupa; a single piece of material, uncut and, in a sense, still alive."

"Oh." Calli hastily let go, allowing the orange garment to settle back on its hanger.

"No, don't worry," the man said, still smiling. "It won't harm you—it's not alive in that sense—and nothing we're doing will hurt it. In adapting the material for clothing all we've done is use it in the way nature intended, more or less. You see, the Selith produce these capes as protection for their young. Feel how warm it is and how strong?" He took up a corner and held it towards Calli. Still a little uncertain, the girl touched the cloth tentatively. It *was* warm, now that Donovan mentioned the fact, and she had already noted its surprising thickness.

"It has to be tough," the man continued, "in order to protect the Selith nymph for the first five years of its life, and adaptable too. We've simply taken advantage of its natural characteristics. You can wear this as a sarong one day, a long-skirted one-piece the next and a short dress the day after that. It's programmed to conform to whatever you choose. In about five years the material will die and disintegrate, but until then it's fire-resistant, almost impossible to cut or tear and will keep you warm and looking beautiful."

She laughed at the blatant flattery. "You make a good salesman."

"I'm glad," the other replied, chuckling himself. "After all, that's what I do."

A sudden thought interrupted her joyful mood. "You don't kill these Seli-thingamyjig nymphs for this stuff, do you?"

"No, you needn't fear on that score," Donovan assured her. "The Selith are the dominant species on Reiggelis; they're sentient. We trade with them for the pupa material. Very expensive it is too, now that they're catching on to just how much it's sought after."

Calli didn't quite buy all this nonsense about other worlds and alien species—nobody ever came back from the colony worlds to Earth anymore—but she loved the story anyway.

"You wouldn't catch me wearing that," said Gemma, who had come over to join them. "I don't want some creepy live thing crawling all over my body, thank you very much."

When put like that, the garment suddenly lost its appeal.

"My dear lady," Donovan responded, "it doesn't crawl, it cuddles." Which sounded much better.

At that point the shopkeeper paused, as if hearing something the two girls had missed. "Ah," he exclaimed, "the new range is ready. If you'll just excuse me for a second." With that he disappeared to the back of the shop.

"See what I mean?" Gemma whispered. "Creepy or what?"

"I think he's kind of sweet."

The two girls lost themselves in browsing through the clothes, marvelling at one garment after another. There was a formal dress with detachable skirt, this one in electric blue but available in a choice of colours. It peeled off to leave a risqué mini-skirt and when reattached, the outfit appeared completely seamless, even under the closest scrutiny. There was a whole rack of self-cleaning trousers in a material that neither girl had encountered before, and Calli was just about to satisfy her curiosity with regard to a display of self-warming underwear when Donovan reappeared.

"Ladies," he said with a flourish, "may I present our latest range."

Two mannequins stepped forward to stand beside him. Eerily lifelike, they adopted catwalk poses and suffered the girls' examination.

One wore a loosely-belted swallow-tail dress, dropping to mid-calf at the back and rising to just above knee-height at the front. It was made from the most beautiful material Calli had ever seen, although she had reservations about the colour—a florally patterned burgundy. The second model wore black trousers and a seamless blouse of the same material, again in burgundy.

"What *is* this?" she asked, mesmerised.

"Silk," Donovan supplied, "a material sadly not seen on Earth in centuries. Our last stop was on Gaynor—a world where the silkworm still thrives, having been taken there by the first colonists. The shop learnt how to spin the material from observing the silkworms and this is our first range to feature it. What do you think?"

"It's lovely..." Calli answered for both of them.

Donovan looked at her intently. "Do I sense a 'but'?"

"Well, it's just the colour..."

"The colour?" He looked astonished. "But burgundy is all the rage, especially on Gaynor."

"Well Gaynor can keep it," Calli told him, a little more sharply than intended. "I mean, I'm sure it's very beautiful, if you're into that sort of thing, but..."

"She's right, you know," Gemma said, backing her friend up. "Stunning material; boring colour. Totally dull."

"Haven't you got it in something brighter?"

"Pastels, you mean?" Donovan studied the mannequins with a speculative eye.

"Anything, just so long as it's not burgundy." Calli knew she was making a lousy job of expressing herself, so tried again. "This material is so gorgeous, it deserves something more vibrant."

"You know, young madam, I think you might have a point." The shopkeeper looked at her with renewed respect. "You really do have a good eye, I saw that straight away. Have you ever considered a career in fashion?"

Calli's buoyant mood abruptly disintegrated, collapsing like a burst bubble.

"Did I say something wrong?" Donovan looked suddenly concerned.

"No, not really." She sighed. "It's just that I've already had my CAT and they've told me what I'm suited to."

"Which is?" the man asked, watching her closely.

"Hydroponics." She spat the word out like a bad taste. "I start the training course next week."

He smiled sympathetically. "You don't appear to be overly enamoured with the prospect. Do you have any great interest in plants or in farming?"

"No; none."

Gemma, who had wandered off to look at clothes again, chipped in with a distracted "Boring."

"It's strange then, don't you think, that the CAT recommends you follow such a career?"

Calli shrugged. "It's what my father does, so I guess it's in the genes."

"Perhaps," the other said, clearly unconvinced. "Tell me, what would you really like to do, if you could do absolutely anything?"

"Travel," she said instantly.

"Where?" he asked. "To other countries, or to the stars?"

Calli was about to answer but stopped herself, wary of saying too much, of revealing her most-guarded dreams. Yet she knew that he could read the answer in her eyes.

"Hey Cal, you *must* see this."

She excused herself and hurried across to see what Gemma had uncovered, relieved to do so. As the two girls continued to explore the shop's wares she forgot her discomfort and almost recaptured the high spirits of earlier. Almost.

In the end Calli bought the Selith sarong—the very first item she had looked at—whilst Gemma bought a couple of skimpy tops and a water-repellent swimsuit. Donovan even gave them a discount as reward for their helpful comments about the new silk range.

"If you come back tomorrow we'll have some silk items in the new 'vibrant' colours for you to try on."

"Great." Calli couldn't wait to feel that wondrous material against her skin. "We'll be here."

"Oh, I almost forgot," he stopped her as they were about to leave. "Take this home and have a look when you get the chance." He handed her an image card. "I've set it at the bit that I think will interest you, but by all means look at the whole thing."

"What is it?"

"Nothing much; it's just an info-prog about the Earth, a sort of travel guide for off-world visitors like me." He smiled that warm smile of his. "I thought you might like to find out what we think of you."

She took the small plastic card, slipped it into a pocket and promptly forgot about it.

"Thanks, Gem," she said to her friend once they were outside.

"Told you it was worth seeing."

"I know, and you were right. I'm really glad you bullied me into coming."

"*Me*, bully *you?*" Gemma cocked her head to one side. "I don't think so!"

GROWING PAINS

Calli grinned. "Maybe not, but thanks anyway." They hugged and parted with a promise to meet again the following day.

On reaching home she went straight to her room, anxious to try on her new garment and to blog about the shop, but she never had the chance.

"Callisandra!"

Calli froze, and knew that she was in trouble. No one other than her mum ever called her *Callisandra* and then only when she had stepped firmly in the manure. She hurried to answer the summons, grabbing the sarong on the way in the vague hope that it might provide a distraction.

Both parents were waiting for her; not a good sign.

"What's this we hear about you going to a new shop today?"

"Oh, that? Sure; Gemma took me. It's really..."

"We would prefer it if you didn't go back there," her father cut in. They would never actually ban her from doing anything, which would be bad parenting, but this was as close as they ever came.

"Why?" She was genuinely astonished. "I mean, it's only a shop."

"Calli, dear, listen to your father."

"Perhaps, but it isn't like any other shop," he said gravely. "This one is dangerous."

"Dangerous? It sells *clothes*, Dad."

"What's that?" he asked, apparently spotting the sarong for the first time. "Is that from the shop?"

"Yes," she said, smiling and holding it out to show them. "See, it's just a..."

Her mum snatched it from her hand. "We'll have nothing like that in *this* house, young lady."

Calli had never seen her mum and dad like this before. It was not so much anger she saw in their eyes, but fear.

All of which gave her plenty to think about later that night. Until the encounter with her parents she had tended to dismiss Donovan's claims of coming from off-world as so much elaborate sales patter, despite the shop's many marvels. After all, he seemed just like a regular guy. A bit eccentric perhaps, but not *alien*. Okay, she knew that people from the colonies were still technically human, but they were not born on Earth, which made them aliens in her book.

She remembered Davy Arthur's warning about the shop being from 'out-of-town', which had so puzzled her at the time since all shops were from out-of-town by definition. She now realised that the words were not intended to be taken literally. The phrase was a euphemism for what he had been afraid to say: 'off-world'.

It seemed that everything Donovan had told her so casually might actually be true. She had stood and nattered about clothes with a man from another world. There were a thousand questions she wanted to ask—should have asked—if only she had taken him seriously.

The stars!

Calli had dreamed of going to the stars and visiting other worlds since she was small. Despite all their centuries of independence, the other worlds were still referred to as 'the colony worlds', when they were mentioned at all. She supposed the vaguely derogatory term helped people to maintain the illusion of Earth's significance, rather than face up to the reality of its true status as an isolated backwater.

It was still hard to believe the reaction of people—people she had known all her life, like Davy Arthur and even her own mum and dad. This was the first time she had ever encountered prejudice, and she found that she didn't like it.

Earth had severed all ties with its precocious children-worlds long ago. Apparently that was a good thing, or so they were told. What did seem certain was that Earth would never again reach out to colonise anywhere. It seemed ironic that the very first colonies were established in the latter half of the so called 'Dark Ages'—the 20th through to the 22nd centuries. Yet the extravagances of that same period had left the Earth so denuded of natural resources that no further exodus from the mother-world would ever be possible, giving the new colonies free rein to claim the stars for themselves.

She had seen images from the Dark Ages; in fact it was required learning for every child. Roads choked with cars and the sky full of planes, all busy converting precious fossil fuel into pollution. What was wrong with the ancestors? Why couldn't they embrace the simple joys of walking? Instead they had exhausted the Earth.

So the stars were out of reach. Visiting other worlds would never be anything more than a dream . . . but what a dream.

Calli fell asleep imagining what it must be like to live like Donovan, seeing all those exotic places and meeting so many different kinds of people.

GROWING PAINS

The next morning found her refreshed and in good spirits. She could hardly wait to visit the shop again and this time intended to go fully prepared with all those questions she had always wanted to ask.

In the cold light of day the confrontation with her parents seemed little more than a bad dream. Already its impact was fading.

She gave Gemma a call first thing, anxious to make arrangements.

"Hello Cal." Her friend looked uncomfortable, embarrassed even.

"You okay?"

"Fine, but look, I won't to be able to make today."

"But what about the shop and trying on all that silk stuff?" Calli realised that she was now in danger of being the one who was pleading.

"Not a good idea. I'm not going near that place again. I told you the old man was creepy, but I never dreamt he was an *alien*."

So she hadn't believed him either.

"Parents?" Calli ventured.

"Heavy-time; yesterday, when I got home."

"Same here."

"Probably for the best. I think the word's out all over town. People are angry."

Angry, or afraid? Clearly it was not just her parents who were overreacting to all of this. By the sound of things, a lot of other people were as well.

"Sorry Cal."

"No probs. We're cool. Talk tomorrow."

She knew there was little love wasted on the colony worlds but still found it hard to accept that feelings ran so deep. Did Donovan have any idea of the amount of resentment building up against his presence? Thinking of him reminded her of the image card he had handed her yesterday. What had she done with it? After a little rummaging around she uncovered the presumably alien card and put it on the console, activating the programme.

An image appeared in the centre of the room—the Earth seen from space. As Donovan had warned, this seemed to be part-way through the programme, but she let it run, curious to find out what he had wanted her to see.

"In the aftermath of the Great Exodus the authorities on Earth became obsessively concerned with stability, with restricting the oppor-

Shop Talk

tunity for change." The unseen narrator's rich tones delivered the commentary with lecture-room precision.

"In theory, the huge advances in AI-based technology that we take so much for granted should enable the citizens of Earth to move around as freely as anyone else, but this has never been the case. The taboos against commuting which first arose in the late 21st century still persist, and society has been structured in many subtle ways to reinforce them.

"The authorities go to extraordinary lengths to provide everything anyone could want as locally as possible, thus avoiding the need for travel." The image switched to that of a typical main street, with shoppers strolling along. "Though no longer a relevant issue, the scarcity of fossil fuels provides a credible excuse for curtailing recreational travel. Where people would once drive to centralised malls or to large cities simply to go shopping, the stores now come to the people. Shops jump from town to town and from city to city, providing a never-ending variety of goods and opportunity for retail therapy.

"Rare on other worlds but common on Earth, the mobile shops are themselves semi-organic constructs, each housing an AI, though on Earth every Intelligence is heavily governed and able to operate only within strictly limited parameters. This remains the only contact that a typical Earthman is ever likely to have with an AI."

Calli sat open-mouthed. This was all new to her. A shop was just a shop; she had never considered what else it might represent.

If the section she had seen so far was a revelation, what followed was even more so. The scene shifted to the image of a girl lying down, with a familiar band of metal around her head.

"Central to the system of control is the Careers Aptitude Test, or CAT, which supposedly examines every individual to the depths of their psyche, determining which career path each person is ideally suited to. The resultant recommendations are adhered to with near-religious faith.

"CAT is a sham, designed to ensure that each person is found a job as close to their home as practicable, with the results tailored to fill vacant niches in the local workforce. This often leads to a trade or occupation being continued within the same family, generation to generation, thus simplifying the whole process.

"An immobile populace is a controllable populace."

GROWING PAINS

Calli was stunned. CAT a *sham*? Yet it made sense. Her greatest dread was the prospect of spending the rest of her life as a hydroponics farmer, yet that was precisely what CAT had decreed for her, what it insisted she was best suited to.

She was not so naïve as to take everything said at face value, but much of what this programme said rang uncomfortably true. One thing was apparent though: prejudices were not just restricted to the people on Earth. Colonials had a few of their own.

The images and the words continued, but she had stopped paying attention, no doubt having already viewed the section that Donovan had intended her to see. She still wanted to watch all of it, but not right now. There were more pressing matters to attend to.

Snatching the info-card from the console, she hurried out of the house and down the lane towards town.

A crowd was gathering on the green by the old school house, including several faces she recognised; Davy and Matt Arthur amongst them. Their mood appeared angry and she ducked down behind the newly-manicured privet hedge and hurried past, anxious not to be seen. Only once she was a little further down the lane did one face in particular register.

Surely that had not been her father?

Another shock awaited her at the clothes shop. Its façade was blackened around the door, as if by soot, and the window stood empty, the strolling mannequin nowhere to be seen. She tried the door, half fearing it would be locked, but it opened straight away.

Donovan was waiting inside and she felt a flood of relief at seeing him unharmed.

"Hello again." His smile now seemed fragile and less certain.

"What happened?"

"Just a spot of bother last night," he gestured dismissively. "Not wholly unexpected, although I had hoped it might take a little longer than this. Somebody tried to burn the shop down."

The horror must have shown on her face. "Is it hurt?"

Donovan smiled. "Not really. Thank you for asking, but there's no need to worry yourself. The shop will heal in no time; look, the window's already regrown."

"It's true then, about the shops being living things, I mean?"

"Oh yes. I thought you might have known that already." He shook his head, "It's very difficult knowing quite what you people here on Earth have been told and what you haven't."

Wordlessly, she held out the image card.

"Ah." He accepted the plastic sliver. "You watched it, then. The question is, did you believe it?"

She hesitated, before nodding slowly.

"And do you still want to be a hydroponics farmer?"

She laughed, a little wearily, and shook her head. "No, I never did."

Suddenly he turned very serious. "Would you like to see the stars, Calli?"

"What?" In a day of shocks, this was the greatest yet. To her dismay she found herself shaking, her head reeling. "Are you serious?"

"That's why I'm here."

"You're here for me?"

"You, or someone very much like you."

He pulled across a chair, which she slumped into gratefully, feeling numb from head to toe.

"It's all right, catch your breath and I'll explain." Another chair materialised and he sat facing her. "Humanity has lost its way, Calli; it may even be dying. Very early stages as yet and it's not apparent to most people, but the process has started.

"The colonies have stopped expanding, you see. In fact they've already begun to draw in on themselves. Pioneer worlds, where life is hard, are being abandoned in favour of the more settled and established planets—the softer option. Why should people struggle to eke out a living when they can live a more comfortable life on one of the inner worlds?

"Without growth a society inevitably stagnates. Earth is a prime example of that; and yet, paradoxically, Earth is also our richest resource: the strongest and purest human gene pool there is. Here humanity's heritage has not been blasted and fractured by exposure to a thousand radiations on as many different worlds, nor warped and bastardised by our own misguided tampering. Here too there is a fierce pride and spirit, even though it is currently suppressed and twisted. We desperately need you for both the purity of your genetic heritage and the ferocity of your spirit, without which humanity may well be doomed. We need the people of Earth to come to the stars, but they don't want to know."

GROWING PAINS

She didn't want to hear any more, feeling like a sponge which had reached saturation point. "I'm sorry, but this is all too much to take in."

"I'm here to find the adventurous ones, the people who long to visit other worlds," Donovan continued. "I'm here to recruit the dreamers; and that's you, isn't it, Calli."

She stared at him in disbelief. "One man? All on your own you're going to gather enough people to save the colonies?"

"Of course not," he said, smiling. "I'm merely the first. Shops like this aren't as common on other worlds as they are here but they're not unknown, and this AI hasn't been restricted in the way that the ones on Earth are. Nor will it just be shops—we're only one of the approaches being considered. I'm here to scout out the possibilities, to test the waters, so to speak."

"Well if this is your idea of being inconspicuous, you've got problems," she said, grinning despite everything.

"It's a dilemma. I don't want to attract too much attention but at the same time I have to announce where I'm from in order to entice the free spirits... and another aspect of my mission is to gauge the reaction that such an incursion evokes from your authorities. Mind you," he admitted with a twinkle in his eye, "perhaps my technique could use a little refinement."

Suddenly they were both laughing.

"Actually, being noticed is essential," he continued as the merriment subsided. "Your government's control relies on ignorance and conditioning. People are angered by my presence because I represent the unknown, because I'm from outside."

Calli nodded. "I saw that in my own mum and dad yesterday."

"Exactly! The anger is just a manifestation of fear, which has its roots in a lack of understanding. Once people realise the implications, once they can see beyond their fear and realise that the stars are not in fact closed to them..." His voice trailed off and for an instant he appeared lost in his own thoughts, as if unable to express the magnitude of what his mind's eye saw.

"Sorry," Calli said, before he could regain the thread of his words, "but I'm having a real problem getting my head around all this." A sudden thought occurred to her. "Are you really a shopkeeper or is this just part of the camouflage?"

"No, no, I genuinely am the custodian of this shop. Everything I told you about Gaynor, Reiggelis, and the Selith is entirely true. I've just been recruited to the cause, so to speak."

Calli felt overwhelmed, unable to think straight. All that she had ever wished for was suddenly being offered to her on a plate, but what about her parents, her friends? For the first time in her life, she had no idea what to do.

"Hydroponics or the stars, Calli; it's up to you."

It was unfair, asking her to make such a decision, to choose between everything she had ever known and everything she had ever dreamed of. "Can I get back to you on this? I really need to think."

A new voice spoke; gentle, feminine tones that seemed to emanate from the air itself. "*I am healed and ready to depart.*"

"I'm afraid that's your answer."

"Was that . . . ?" She could not quite bring herself to complete the question.

He nodded. "The shop, yes. Last night's incident made it clear we've outstayed our welcome. We have only delayed our departure to allow time for full healing and in the hope that you might come back before we left." The man gazed at her, his gaze demanding a decision.

She took a deep breath. "If you're asking me to decide right now, the answer has to be . . . no. I can't commit to something like this on impulse. I just can't." Somewhere deep inside her, hope withered and died.

Donovan slumped. "I understand. But you're making a mistake." His voice was small, defeated.

A familiar deep vibration began.

"I know," she whispered and meant it, even as she stood and proceeded to walk out of the shop on unsteady legs, tears stinging her eyes.

To find herself confronted by an angry mob, led by Matt Davy.

"Calli?"

Her unexpected appearance gave them pause but she could almost smell the fear and the rage that emanated from the crowd, whilst her eyes registered clenched fists, clubs, the glint of steel, and hate-filled expressions all around. United by their prejudice, they had assumed the aspect of a single organism blindly reacting to a perceived threat, rather than a group of reasoning individuals.

GROWING PAINS

"What do you think you're doing here, young lady? I told you to stay away from this shop!"

"Dad?" So it *had* been her father she saw with them at the old school house. How could *he* be a part of something like this, how could any of them? Rage welled-up inside her. Suddenly, these were not the people she knew anymore.

Hydroponics or the stars . . . the anger of the mob or the comfort of the shop . . . .

The shop was about to go, its tell-tale whine building rapidly. She whipped around and threw herself at the door, hoping against all reason that it would still open.

For a brief instant it seemed to resist her, but then gave inward and she fell inside, into the arms of the ever-smiling Donovan, who helped her to a chair.

The whine reached a peak and suddenly cut off. She guessed they were on their way. It was strange, she had seen shops vanish a hundred times, but had never been inside one when it did. There was no sense of movement, just a peculiar calm.

Donovan was laughing and hopping from foot to foot, almost doing a jig in his excitement and delight.

"*Welcome, Calli,*" said the serene but nebulous voice of the AI. "*You are the first. The first of many.*"

Calli felt exhilarated, buoyant, in total contrast to the despondency that had engulfed her a moment earlier when she thought she was walking away from her dreams forever.

The first of many . . . ? That sounded good. In fact, that sounded very good.

Calli saw again the hate in the faces of the mob, in the eyes of people she knew and loved, and determined to do all she could to wipe away such fear and ignorance.

Only then would she feel free to come home again.

The Piano Song

Kimberly Hobson was coming home; perhaps in the only way she ever *could* have come home.

Her mother's death had left her feeling oddly hollow. There was sadness, but only associated with the realisation that this marked an end in many senses—she was truly alone now. Her dad had gone first, claimed by lingering cancer which had made him feel he was being 'evicted from his own body by a usurper'. Those were his own words, spoken in a tone of frustrated injustice which she would never forget. And then Ed—killed in a head-on collision with a truck three years ago. Always cheerful, always there: Ed, her brother, who had been the one remaining link to the childhood she remembered. At least he'd gone quickly, or so the police assured her.

Now it was the turn of her mother, who had never really been a link to anything. Her death was difficult to accept—not for any deep-rooted emotional reason, but because Kim had somehow assumed that her mum would go on forever; this woman her father once referred to affectionately as 'a force of nature', though Kim had always seen her more as feature of the landscape—a rocky outcropping, a mountain that blocked the view, refused to give ground and was impossible to get around.

Kim took a series of deep breaths and started to walk up the gravel drive. She'd parked on the road—a habit she couldn't break even now for some reason. Driving onto the property itself felt wrong, a trespass too far.

Why did this whole business make her want to reach for a cigarette that wasn't there? She had given up years ago, but right now would have killed for a smoke. A betraying hand had sneaked into her bag before

GROWING PAINS

she could stop it; she quickly converted the action into a general rummage, as if to kid herself that the thought of cigarettes had never even entered her mind. Questing fingers closed on something; a packet of mints.

Her feet stumbled to a halt as she drew the mints out, leaving her to simply stare at the house—this brooding presence that squatted there, waiting for her, a Pandora's Box of her past. Kim wished there was someone to come with her, someone she could lean on for support and look to share this ordeal with, but there wasn't. Paul had been excised from her life nearly ten years ago—no children and a swift divorce. Since then there'd been the occasional man, she'd 'dated' from time to time and had even slept with one or two, but none of these transient companions had touched her in a meaningful way and she'd always sidestepped anything that threatened to become a relationship, even Damon, who had been besotted and pursued her stubbornly for a while.

None of them had been allowed as close as Paul, and no one ever would be again.

In a way, she didn't even blame the girl. Mandy was a slut, always had been, even at school. She went through men like crisp packets, picking them up, emptying them and then chucking them away before moving onto the next one.

"Look out, girls, here comes Mandy; we'd better lock our husbands up," wasn't even something they whispered behind her back, it was something she laughed about with them.

No, she couldn't entirely blame Mandy, but Paul was another matter. If he were going to betray her with anyone, why did it have to be Mandy Gibson of all people? So blonde, so busty, and so fucking *obvious*.

In truth, she felt nearly as annoyed at her own missed opportunities as she did at Paul's actual betrayal. She remembered Martin from work; tall, buff Martin. The office party—now how was that for a cliché?—when it would have been so easy to succumb to the alcohol, his flattery, his attention, and her own desires. Yet she'd resisted, because she was married, because of *Paul*. One kiss; that was all they'd shared; that and the feeling of his impressive erection pressing against her midriff. The temptation was there, raging inside her, the desire to abandon caution and go with the flow, to reach down and caress that bulge, to cling to him and demand that he took her, that he satisfied her, but instead she'd broken the clinch, stepped away and told him that she couldn't; that she was married and this must never happen again. In defiance of her own racing heart and mounting lust, she stayed loyal.

Not that her abstinence had prevented her from feeling guilty as hell for months afterwards, causing her to work her socks off to be the best wife she could possibly be, desperate that Paul should never suspect her of that one stolen kiss. A *kiss*? And there was her precious husband banging Mandy Gibson's brains out hard enough to break the bloody bed!

The fact that she'd fought so hard to stay faithful while he'd rolled over and screwed the first slut who batted her false eyelashes at him was something she would never *ever* forgive him for.

She slipped a mint into her mouth and instantly wished she hadn't. Whatever a mint was, it was no substitute for a cigarette. The headache that had plagued her since first waking that morning threatened to get worse; a persistent throb of pain somewhere behind the eyes. She tried to ignore it and sucked hard on the mint.

The house was exactly as she remembered: flat-faced, pebble dashed, imposing, and *big*. Someone had stripped the ivy away from around the door and never repainted, leaving a brown tattoo of the plant's former presence on the wall, looking as if all the colour and substance had somehow been leached out of the paint and the brickwork where the creepers touched. That was about the only variance from the picture memory provided.

The door was just the same—solid wood and in need of a coat of varnish—while the cold metal of the key in her hand felt oddly awkward and out of place.

It was still hard to accept her mother's death as real, despite the funeral, the lawyers, the reading of the will and the abundance of black—they were things experienced by someone else, which she had merely observed.

There ought to have been more grief, but the truth was Kim had been mourning her mother for nearly nine years. They'd only seen each other once in that time—at Ed's funeral—and spoken no more than twice since, so her current sense of loss was minimal. Would it have been different if Mum had died first? Probably; she had always been a daddy's girl and would almost certainly have stayed close to her father had he been the surviving parent. Her mother on the other hand was a

GROWING PAINS

calculating bitch, a manipulator, wrapped up in her own version of how the world should be and determined to make life adapt to her vision rather than the other way around.

Particularly as regards her daughter's husband.

When Kim first suspected that her mother's hand had been involved in Paul's infidelity, she went ballistic. The worst part was that the old shrew refused to either confirm or deny any involvement, insisting that her daughter shouldn't even think to make such an accusation.

The problem was that it would have been *so* like Mother to feign illness that weekend, knowing that Kim would come across and stay to look after her, while making sure that Mandy knew Paul was alone and suggesting she should pop in to check how well he was coping. That was Mandy's subsequent claim, and the more Kim mulled it over the more she tended to believe the slut.

Mum had disapproved of Paul from the start; not her choice of son-in-law at all.

Kim never did find out who her mother had lined up as replacement; by then, they weren't talking to each other.

The key slid into the ubiquitous Yale lock and Kim found herself hesitating. For some reason, she felt more trepidation about this moment than she had about any of it to date. Taking a deep breath, she turned the key and pushed. Brief resistance from the accumulated junk mail, which fanned out to form an irregular mat as she forced the door inward, then she was stepping inside.

Perhaps in retrospect she shouldn't have been surprised by what then happened. After all, she was receptive from the moment the door opened. As Kim stood there on the threshold of that old house and of her childhood, it was with a sense of expectation, as if she were simply waiting for the memories to wash over her, to swamp her, to carry her along on a wave of nostalgia all the way back to the girl she'd once been—her and Ed running along this hallway, laughing. Fun; that was another member of the family she'd become estranged from in recent years. When exactly had she forgotten how to have fun?

Yet none of that happened, not immediately. At first the house felt lifeless, as if anything connected to her had seeped away long ago. She struggled to feel something, to connect with this place that had been her home for so many years, and failed. Then came the music. Not distinctly, not pervasively, but distant and half-heard, as if someone had left the radio on in another room. The piano. She strained to hear, recognising the song immediately. A dam broke inside her and all the memories came flooding back: that song... her song. No words, it didn't need lyrics; the rhythmic, melodic flow of notes spoke more poignantly than any verse man could ever articulate.

She sobbed, and was surprised to find tears welling up from the recesses of her eyes. *How could she have forgotten her song?*

Kim always assumed the haunting, rippling theme was something she had heard, perhaps on the radio; a snatch of tune that had connected to some element of her young mind and lodged there, but in all the years that intervened she had never managed to track it down, never succeeded in identifying that simple yet so effective melody. Never heard it *anywhere* except in her own head.

Mind you, that in itself amounted to hearing the song more frequently than any other piece of music. This tune, which she'd come to think of as simply *The Piano Song* for want of anything more definite, had provided the soundtrack to her childhood.

It was there when she played with her toys, when she read her books, when she was out somewhere with family or friends. As Barbie changed clothes for the third time in almost as many minutes, or sat wondering why Ken didn't take more notice of her, she'd be humming the tune in her head. When Kim's Pippa Dolls sat in their cardboard house on furniture made from matchboxes, yoghurt pots, sticky-back plastic and pipe cleaners—all based on designs taught her during recent episodes of *Blue Peter*—it was *her* tune that issued from the record player. As Mary Lennox nurtured *The Secret Garden*, she did so with *The Piano Song* playing in the background, and it was against this haunting melody that she first heard Colin Craven's weeping. When Lucy first tumbled out of the wardrobe and found herself in the magical realm of Narnia, there was only one tune that could possibly have accompanied her.

And as the adolescent Kim walked along a forest path, disdaining Ed's jibes and his yells for her to hurry up, *The Piano Song* added texture to the dappled sunlight, the sighing of the leaves in the gusting breeze, the distant bleating of sheep from somewhere beyond the trees, the sporadic birdsong, and the faint scent of wood smoke carried on the wind. The scene would have been beautiful without the music, but was complete only with it.

GROWING PAINS

The adult Kim walked down a dark, carpeted hallway and imagined it was leaf mould and earth beneath her shoes; but she didn't have to dredge up memories of *The Piano Song*; it was there in her head, just as clear and beautiful as ever.

She wondered whether Mother had kept the piano. A grand—not a Steinway perhaps, but neither was it an electronic keyboard made of moulded plastic with pre-programmed rhythms and dozens of different voices. A *real* piano; a gracefully curved wonder in polished rosewood, with the words 'John Broadwood & Sons, London' inscribed in flowing script above the ivory keys. She didn't care that it was valuable, didn't care that it was rare. It was hers, and that was far more important.

The first door, on her left as she drew level with the stairs, led to the dining room. Kim's hand hovered over the handle for a moment, as she worried what memories might be pent-up inside waiting to pounce, but then she grasped and turned. The room smelt of stale polish and mustiness. How many times had it seen use in the past nine years? A dozen, perhaps? In truth she doubted if it was even that often. When left to her own devices her mum invariably ate meals in the lounge, in front of the TV, with a cushioned tray balanced precariously on her lap. On the rare occasions she entertained friends the kitchen table earned its keep. But the dining room? That was reserved only for 'special occasions'. The room's purpose had become eroded and diminished with the passage of time and changing lifestyles, until it was finally reduced to being what, a status symbol? A nostalgic memory of the distant days when everyone had been expected to gather there for the ritual of 'the family meal'?

Kim shivered and shut the door. She never had been especially keen on the dining room or the furniture trapped within.

But the song was still there.

The hall grew dimmer as she walked farther into the house. Had it always been this dark in here? Memory suggested otherwise. And the song swelled around her, lightening her feet and easing the headache.

The piano had been bought for her. Not *entirely* for her (after all, what better status symbol could there be than having a grand piano in the house?), but primarily so. Ed had never been bothered about playing the piano. Kim wanted to learn, was *desperate* to learn; so that she could play her tune: *The Piano Song*.

She walked straight past the lounge, making her way to the far end of the hallway and the door that stood straight ahead of her. Had the song ever sounded so loud? Doubtful. It seemed that, after being neglected for so many years, the tune was determined that she should *never* forget again. She was approaching it fast now, that door.

As a child, Kim had suffered from a low attention span—something which continued to plague her throughout her life, though it proved to be less of an issue as she grew older. Learning the piano took time; it required dedication and patience—qualities that Kim lacked in abundance. She gave up, exasperated by her inability to master the instrument overnight and annoyed with herself for not persisting. Kim knew that only her yearning to play that one song had kept her going for as long as she had, until long after it became obvious that she would never reach the standard necessary to actually master the stupid instrument. This realisation drove her to long sessions of sitting by herself at the piano, playing notes in ones and twos and threes, trying to find the proper sequence, to match the sounds her fumbling fingers created to the lilting beauty that tripped through her head. Once or twice she even thought she had something, but in the end these solo sessions too led only to frustration.

No one else in the house seemed bothered with playing the piano, but, as far as Kim knew, it was still here.

She heard the tune so clearly now; surely it wasn't just in her head. Kim rarely felt the need for anyone, but right then she wished there was someone beside her who could say, "Yes, I can hear it too." But there was only her.

It sounded for all the world as if somebody were actually *playing* it; her tune. Right here and right now—playing with an effortless surety that she could only envy, yet using her piano to do so. For the music was coming from just beyond this door, she was sure of it. Kim took a deep breath and reached for the handle. As she did so, a fresh spasm of pain blossomed in her head. What the hell was going on? She'd never been one for headaches before.

Then, the oddest thing; the door handle seemed to shift, to jump, almost as if trying to avoid her, to escape her touch. The illusion passed in an instant and her fingers fastened around the handle. For a moment she simply gripped the cold metal, squeezing it firmly, as if making sure it was real, that it was solid and not inclined to turn insubstantial and slip away from her grasp.

Still the music drew her on.

GROWING PAINS

Kim turned the handle and pushed the door open.

Light flooded the hallway, causing her to squint. Suddenly she realised why the place had seemed so dark earlier—because of this door. Had she ever seen it closed before? Not that she could think of, except perhaps in the winter, at night, when it might be shut to keep the heat in. Otherwise, the door had always stood open, allowing light into this back-end of the house. Amazing what a difference such a simple thing could make.

The music never faltered.

She stepped into the room, dazzled by the light and the sound. There was her piano, looking exactly as she remembered . . . and there was a young girl, not yet a teen, sitting at the piano and playing. Playing her song.

But of course—what else would she be playing? After all, the young girl was *her*, as she'd been when she was, what, twelve? No, eleven—she remembered that dress, how much she'd hated the patterning of bright flowers set against a black background. Funny, it struck her as perfectly okay now—pretty in a prim and proper sort of way—but to her eleven-year old self it had been the ultimate humiliation to have to wear such a sombre, dreary thing, for all that her mother insisted it was 'smart and lovely'. This was the dress she was required to wear when her parents had 'guests'—smiling elderly faces to whom she and Ed were to be presented. Lord, how she loathed them—Mum and guests the same. Not Dad, of course, who seemed oblivious to how awful this all was for her. She was certain that he would have put a stop to such performances if only he'd realised. Yet never certain enough to actually test the theory by asking him to.

Kim watched in awe as the fingers of her girlhood self danced across the keyboard, playing her song as she had always dreamed of doing, as she had always yearned to do. She felt a great upwelling of joy as she realised that she *could* play this, that she had always been able to, that the music was inside of her, a part of her.

She blinked away tears, and knew this to be the happiest, proudest moment of her life.

The girl-that-was-her looked up, smiling, and invited Kim to join her with a shallow nod and a movement of the eyes. The woman sat on the stool beside this apparition from her past, and, after watching for a few careful moments, felt confident enough to join in. Her playing was effortless, unhesitating, the music seeming to flow through her, spreading out to inhabit every corner of body and soul, directing her unpractised fingers. She closed her eyes, the tears running freely now, soft and warmly ticklish where they trailed down her cheeks. Somewhere along the way the girl had left or disappeared, leaving her to play the song, *her* song, alone. And it was beautiful.

Without warning the headache returned, but more, much more. She gasped, blinded by agony. Her fingers faltered, the song died . . .

A month after her mother passed away, the body of Kimberley Jeanette Hobson was discovered in the music room of her old family home. Found to have died of a brain aneurism, the broad smile on her features was put down to the effect of *rigor mortis* acting on the muscles of her face.

Her funeral was a quiet affair, with less than a dozen people showing up to pay their respects—her ex-husband unable to attend due to work commitments. Among those few who were present was an old school friend of the deceased: one Mandy Gibson.

Mandy had no real idea why she had come, except that she'd always regretted the loss of Kim's friendship and felt compelled to attend, perhaps to say goodbye, and perhaps to say 'sorry' with a sincerity she'd never quite managed while Kim was alive.

The sparseness of mourners saddened her; Kim deserved better.

At the funeral, as the coffin disappeared towards its fiery end, a rather lovely piece of music played over the sound system: a simple piano tune, rhythmic, haunting and melancholic, yet beautiful. It seemed entirely appropriate somehow, both for the occasion and for Kim. Mandy had never heard the tune before but instantly found herself humming its theme quietly as she walked out. She determined to ask someone what it was.

Of course, she never did, though the tune stayed with her.

She decided to think of it simply as *The Piano Song*.